Short fiction and
chapter of the League or Utah Writers

IF NOT NOW,
WHEN?

This book is a work of fiction. Names, characters, places, and incidents either are products of the authors' imagination or are used fictitiously. Any resemblance to actual events or locales or persons, living or dead, is entirely coincidental and not intended by the authors.

Copyright © 2021 by Genre Writers Infinite Monkeys Corporation
Cover art © 2021 by Genre Writers Infinite Monkeys Corporation
Cover art design by Rebecacovers
Managing Editor: Talysa Sainz
Edited by: Talysa Sainz, Terra Luft, Daniel Yocom and Johnny Worthen
Layout and Interior Design by Johnny Worthen

ISBN-13: 978-1-7325836-3-4 (paperback)
ISBN-13: 978-1-7325836-2-7 (ebook)

Library of Congress Control Number: 2021910929

"UnVeiled" © 2021 by J.T. Moore
"Still Frame" © 2021 by Rhiannon Carswell
"Raven the Third" © 2021 by Talysa Sainz
"Time Machines Only Go One Way" © 2021 by John M. Olsen
"Monochromatic" © 2021 by Danielle Harward
"Intertwined" © 2021 by Holly Voss
"Mended" © 2021 by Amanda Hill
"The Last Chance" © 2021 by Johnny Worthen
"Pioneering Final Frontiers" © 2021 by C. H. Lindsay
"Bioengineering the End of the World" © 2021 by Bradley S. Blanchard
"Tillicum" © 2021 by Scott E. Tarbet
"Bag Lady" © 2021 by Gail Boling
"Conviction" © 2021 by Daniel Yocom
"Time to Go" © 2021 by Terra Luft
"Wild Bunch Barber" © 2021 by Bryan Young

All rights reserved. Except as permitted under the U.S. Copyright Act of 1976, no part of this publication may be reproduced, distributed, or transmitted in any form or by any means, or stored in a database or retrieval system, without the prior permission.

First paperback edition: July 2021

CONTENTS

Introduction

by Terra Luft

You're holding in your hand more than a collection of stories and poetry. It is that, of course, but it's also physical, tangible proof of the resilience of those whose work is contained within these pages. Also known as members of The Infinite Monkeys. Who could have predicted back in 2019 when we set out on this great adventure to produce our second anthology as a writing group that the world was poised on the precipice of a pandemic? Thanks to COVID-19, 2020 was an unprecedented year of stress and isolation, with an extra dash of social upheaval. Yet we stayed the course, pushing each other to create and persevere, improving and perfecting our craft, and chasing our dreams despite it all. Even when we only saw each other in virtual meetings instead of in person twice a month. Even when the mere effort of day-to-day existence was wearisome. Even when the state of the world tried to squash our spirits and steal the creativity from us. Why? Because like the title and theme of this collection suggest, if not now, when? To all the authors who answered the call for submissions, and the leadership team who also moonlighted as editing staff and publishing house, I'm proud of us all!

To you, our readers, who have honored us by picking up this book, I thank you and am excited for you to explore the stories and poetry presented here. You'll find award-winning authors and newcomers alike across many genres, including science fiction, romance, western, fantasy, historical, paranormal, and horror. Hopeful, triumphant, dark, and fanciful all await you within these pages. You, dear reader, are our best reason to keep writing. I hope you finish entertained and that—no matter what—you keep reading.

To all "my Monkeys," past and present, it has been my honor to lead this amazing writing group for the last five years. This is dedicated to you. It is bittersweet that helping bring this book into existence is also my final act as your president. You all inspire me. I hope that—no matter what—you keep writing. There's no time like the present to chase dreams. Because if not now, when? Finally, to the amazing humans who have walked this leadership path with me—Johnny Worthen (who is to blame for all of it), Talysa Sainz, Alex Jay Lore, and Daniel Yocom—I couldn't have done any of it without you, nor would I have wanted to with anyone else.

~ Terra Luft, President (2016-2021)
The Infinite Monkeys
A Chapter of the League of Utah Writers

Short fiction and poetry by the Infinite Monkeys chapter of the League of Utah Writers

IF NOT NOW,
WHEN?

IF NOT NOW, *WHEN?*

UnVeiled

by J.T. Moore

He walked into the diner for a to-go cup of coffee. Leda Johnson would never be able to identify his face but she knew it was him. His green and brown aura was smudged and the shadow riding his back was a dead giveaway. She had seen him twice a day, every day for the past week and it was with him every time. He was nervous and he should be. He was going to die. Maybe not today or tomorrow but real soon. She hated knowing this but more than that, she hated her hesitation, the fear that kept her quiet, kept her from offering help. Again.

She sat in the booth at her favorite corner diner, her milk-white eyes hidden behind a pair of dark shades and her cane resting beside her against the wall. Her thick, curly hair was pulled into a puff showing off her warm brown skin and full lips. The smell of coffee and bacon permeated everything in a make-your-stomach-growl kind of way. The server cleared her empty plate and brought her another coffee. Her fingers found the rim of the cup, she added cubes of sugar and cream, her fingers inside the edge of the cup so she wouldn't overfill.

The music of the New York streets, noisy with traffic and commuters on this mild fall day, wasn't enough to lift her spirits like it usually would. The diner was a temporary haven. Stevie Wonder's newest hit, *Living for the City,* playing in the background, was interrupted by the louder street sounds every time the door opened. She waited. Right on time, the cop entered as the future dead man left.

"Good morning, Officer." The waitress greeted him every morning with a smile in her voice.

His aura of black, blue, and yellow with an overall sheen radiated trust, calm, and the possible touch of a mystic in a room full of frenetic rainbow people whose sole focus was on themselves. She had watched the cop off and on for the past few weeks. Maybe she would do it today and not care what he thought of a blind woman who saw auras and talked to dead people.

She could make out vague impressions and shadows of the real world, but death and the ghosts they left behind were very clear. She couldn't tell the other man she had seen his death. The last time she tried to tell any-one she was seven and had told the neighbor there was a little monster riding on her back. The neighbor told Leda's mom who had a serious talk with Leda about how she couldn't tell anyone about the things she saw. That lady also told Leda's mom that they should send Leda to the 'special school'. Her mom put the fear of God in that woman for saying her daughter was anything other than a smart little girl. The woman died three days later. A stroke, they said. Leda promised her mother she would never do it again. So she hadn't. She spent her life ignoring anything she could see clearly because she knew that meant no one else could.

Leda saw the warm aura of the cop at the counter, the cold metal of his gun dull in the ether. He was greeted by name, the subtle change in the cashier's voice, flirty, as she took his order for coffee, black. She needed someone who would not think she was crazy when she finally said how she knew someone was about to die. It was now or never. She gathered her cane in one hand and with her other, slid the strap of her book bag over her shoulder cross-body style. She held the almost full cup of coffee in her free hand.

The bump and spill of coffee on the cop looked like an accident. It wasn't. "Oh I'm sorry, I didn't know you were standing there."

"Whoa sister, are you blind?" She heard the smile behind the statement.

"Yes, actually." She wiggled the cane out in the general direction of his voice.

"Oh shit, um sorry."

"It's okay, really. I'm the one who's sorry. I was just on my way to school and didn't want to be late." She tucked the cane beneath an arm and held out a hand. "I'm Leda Johnson, and I hope I didn't burn you."

"No, I'm fine, most of it hit the floor. I'm Officer Michael Lancaster."

"I'm a teacher for the blind." She cleared her throat and went for it. "Can I talk to you about something, semi-official?"

"Let me get my coffee and I'll walk with you."

"Perfect. Thank you." If she didn't know that he was a black man before, the 'sister' gave it away. Also, she could tell by his voice, which was deep and resonated in her soul. She was done hiding what she could do, maybe she could actually help someone. If not, at least she would try. She had to tell somebody, damn the consequences. If she didn't do something now what was the point. New York in the '70s was all about black power, hers was just a different type of power. The kind people feared.

They walked down the crowded sidewalk in companionable silence without bumping into anyone and miraculously without Leda getting her cane caught in a subway grate. The smell of exhaust, smoke, and the numerous carts of dirty water dogs, the best hotdogs anywhere, surrounded them. She used the time to find the words that would make him take her seriously. She hoped.

"I have a confession to make." It came out tentative, breathless, and hopeful. "A man is going to die, I think he is going to be murdered, I don't know when or how just that he is."

"And how do you know this?" The flatness and lack of emotion in the question made her wary. People got that way before they told her to get away from them. She ploughed on anyway, too late to stop now.

"He has a rider, my term, like a small creature on his back. She hesitated. "A ghost. It's waiting to collect him."

He stopped in the middle of the sidewalk, touched her hand so she would stop too. The grumbling and the disturbance of air against her skin increased as people went around them. "Do you know who is going to kill him?

"No."

"How can I believe you?"

"I don't have an answer for that other than to ask you to trust me. He doesn't have much longer."

"Then why tell me?"

"Because I'm sick of knowing things like this and not being able to help." She threw one hand in the air, the cane in her other hand hitting against his shoe. "At least this way if we can't prevent it maybe I can help you find

4

his killer." This was her last chance, if she couldn't get him to believe her she didn't know if she would have the nerve to approach anyone again. Ever. If not now . . .

"Are you a root worker or something?"

That threw her, but it was also a good sign. "What do you know about roots?" Root doctors or workers were healers and conjurers, good and bad, among southern black people. The term used by the majority population was voodoo and it was more real than they ever knew.

"Southern grandmother," he said.

She released a breath. "Ain't that the truth?" That was probably where the touch of a mystic came from, a slight sheen to his aura where someone put a protection over him.

"But how does it help our potential victim?"

"If you're willing, that's what I'm hoping you can help me with." She reached out again, this time with a light touch on his arm, the fabric of his uniform shirt crisp with light starch. "Can you meet at the diner after work this evening?"

Leda was waiting inside the door when he came in. The guy with the rider would be by soon. She had only noticed the rider this week, otherwise she would have ignored him as she had the others. The city was a big place with lots of people, there was always a spirit or an essence floating around trying to recapture a life ended. This one just felt violent, not like he was ill or anything. It was not good or evil just purposeful.

"There he is." She pointed in the general direction of the rider. His rider was close, bright and hungry in its eagerness.

They left the shop and followed him.

"I have my badge and notified backup. Told them I'm following a tip. Mine if I ask you something?"

"You're out here with me, following a man because I asked you to, so no I don't mind."

"This thing you do. What is it and how does it work?"

"I was born veiled, or en caul, still inside the amniotic sac. When the midwife cut it away, my eyes were shockingly white. At least that's what my mama told me. I was also blind. She said they would walk into my room and I would be laughing like I was responding to someone. I guess I was. I can see shapes some color in people's auras, but not much definition. But ghosts and things from the other side are very clear to me."

"That's . . ."

"Weird. I know." She dipped her head and turned away from" him.

"No. I was going to say damn cool."

She smiled in the direction of his voice and they kept walking. "So why did you agree to help me?"

"For now, let's just say I'm curious. My grandmother told me that just because I can't see something doesn't mean it can't exist."

They tailed the guy with the rider for a few blocks, just a couple out for a stroll. Leda's hand rested on Michael's arm.

"Curb," he said.

He was a natural. He asked first if he could guide her then made a point to tell her if there were obstacles in her path. He was impressive, which was why she was surprised when he left her amid the screech of tires.

She stood there for a moment as the shocked gasps of people surrounded her. She didn't know if it was safe to move but swept her cane in front of her just in case.

"Leda," Michael called, "you're good where you are." He came back and told her that their guy had almost gotten hit by a car.

"Is he okay?"

"Yes, just a little shaken."

She turned her head until she spotted the rider. "No change." She put her hand back on his arm. "He's still going to die."

They followed him for days. She felt ridiculous and decided to tell Michael that they should stop. She hated wasting his time. She would end this tonight when he walked her home, but tonight's trip had already begun.

She was about to ask him why he was doing this when someone stepped out of the dark alley behind the man they were following.

"Stay here," Michael said.

The sound of his footsteps running away goaded her. "The hell I will." She walked faster using her cane to avoid obstacles. She wore tennis shoes with her bell-bottom pants but running was something she usually avoided. She tripped anyway—fell and scraped her palm as garbage-scented water splashed her face and clothes. Gagging, she levered herself up to her knees and felt around for her cane.

A voice startled her. "To your left." The voice was young, a teen on the edge of adulthood. Where did he come from?

"You need to leave," she told the boy. "Something bad is about to go down."

"I know." The boy said. "You should hurry, the way is clear and your boyfriend is hurt."

"He's not . . . Never mind." But she wondered, briefly. The shouting got louder.

A gunshot echoed, and running footsteps faded down the alley.

"Stop now." The boy said. "He's in front of you."

Her cane bumped something soft. She got down on her knees and ran her hands over Michael's body.

"I'm okay, I'm okay. He just knocked me down for a minute." She felt his hand touch her arm. "Are you okay?"

She nodded. In the distance, she could hear sirens and the whoop of the ambulance. The boy was standing over the man they had been following. She crawled over to him just inside the mouth of the garbage-strewn alley and tried to find a pulse. The rider didn't look at her, just reached into the body and pulled. The soul was bright and confused. He had an inner glow that didn't show in this world. The rider tugged him into the distance before the body expelled its last breath. She wished she knew where they were taken. She didn't know the guy but was sad for him and mad at herself that she didn't stop it. What good was having this thing/gift whatever when she couldn't help.

"Leda?" The teen was next to her. "I gotta go, he's getting away."

"Wait, where are you going?"

"Leda, who are you talking to?" Michael said.

"The kid, right here." She waved to her right.

"Umm, Leda, there's no one else here."

The teen shrugged.

"Well hell," she said. She had ignored all ghosts since she was a teen trying to fit in, and they had stopped trying to get her attention.

"What?"

"Ghost, that's what. Couldn't be no more than seventeen. The ghost held up eight fingers. "Eighteen," she finished.

"Where did he go?" she asked the ghost.

The ghost pointed.

"Down that way," Leda repeated.

Michael ran down the alley. "Wait here."

Again with the wait here crap. Ain't gonna happen.

By the time Leda exited the other end of the alley, Michael was yelling at someone to stay down. "Leda, don't come any closer."

She barely heard him, but she took a few steps backward. At least they had turned the sirens off. People on the street gathered around as she heard officers telling them to step back. Of course they didn't listen. She heard Michael say 'she's with me' before he said her name. She stopped moving as her foot crunched on something hard. She reached down to pick up a small round object, her finger traced an engraving on the front. "What is this?" she asked when Michael was closer. She handed him the object.

"It's a pocket watch. Where did you find it?"

"Here. She pointed down to her foot. "I stepped on it."

Someone called to Michael. One of the other officers dealing with the suspect. "Give me a minute to take care of this. I'll be right back."

"Will they say anything about you doing your job out of uniform?"

"Maybe, but I have my badge where they can see it. I need to go help with this then look for the person who was with him. Look, I know we haven't known each other long, but I am just awed at what you can do." He touched her hand lightly. "I'll be back."

Leda turned back the way she had come, going to check on the guy they had been following. Considering the fact that he was now dead, she really didn't know what else to do. The ambulance was there for the dead guy and the cops were talking to any other witnesses. She didn't hear much noise. Smart people usually flee at the sound of gunshots.

The cops had the first suspect and they had no idea where the other one had gone. They talked to her, she couldn't give them a visual but she answered their questions and gave her number. This was now a crime scene and she would have to wait for Michael or go home and call him later to let him know she was okay.

The night was cooler the way it gets in early fall. She was happy for her windbreaker. She made her way back down the alley, her cane sweeping her way forward though she would have to disinfect it after this.

Halfway down, she stopped. Standing in front of her was the young man from earlier. Now that she was paying attention she noticed what she hadn't before. The dirty bell-bottom jeans and the blood surrounding the hole in the middle of his chest. She opened her mouth to tell him her name when he put his fingers to his lips in a shushing motion. He pointed a few feet in front of her and to her left. "There's a man hiding behind the dumpster waiting for you to walk by," he said.

"Was he one of the guys who killed the man in the alley?"

"He was with him, and he is hiding, so he probably just wants to escape."

Leda wasn't sure what to do. She could keep walking and pretend she didn't know he was there. That was probably the easiest, her white cane making that more than believable. Running back to Michael and the other cops would flush him out but someone would get hurt, most likely her. She wouldn't be able to run fast enough to get away or even know which way to go. Her best solution would be to continue and hope he didn't see her as someone who would flush him out, or a helpless victim.

She made sure to tap her cane on the bricks a few times instead of sweeping it in front of her. If he was hiding she wanted him to ignore her, people were good at that.

She exited the alley and stood with the group of people milling around the stoop in the aftermath of all the excitement.

The ghost came up and stood in front of her. "He's walking out. What do you want to do?"

"Follow him, of course. I'll call Michael when we know where he's going"

"Okay, how are we going to do this? You can't hold on to my arm or anything."

"Just walk in front of me, go around or hop over any obstacles and I can follow you. Call out the cross streets so I can relay it to Michael."

Once the guy left the area he sped up. Too fast for Leda to keep up but the ghost would follow and come back.

"What's your name?" She asked him.

"Lance."

"So Lance, why haven't you moved on, you haven't asked me to help you but if you're still here that tells me you have some unfinished business."

"I'm just watching over my little brother, trying to keep him out of trouble and in school where he belongs," he said. "We're crossing West 105th street."

"Why did you decide to help us?"

"You look like you needed it, and I've been following this guy for a while." He pointed. He went into that bodega and out the back. There's a fire escape he used to get to a shitty apartment on the third floor."

"Why, and is there a payphone around here?" She left a message with the address at the precinct for Michael. "How do you know about his apartment?"

Lance ignored her question. "He's gonna split, we need to get up there."

"And do what?"

"Find a way to keep him up there until your cop friend gets here."

"If you haven't realized it yet, I'm blind and you're a ghost. A crime-fighting duo we do not make."

"Well, we can. If you let me in."

"Let you in where."

"If you let me use your body, I will have a physical body and you would be able to see through my eyes."

She laughed. "You've got to be kidding, if you think I'm going to let you--"

"So how else are you going to get him? He knows they'll be looking for him and he's dumping evidence and getting ready to split.

"How do you know what he's doing?"

"I followed him."

"Right. Dammit, okay, how does it work? "

"You've never done this?"

"Of course not, why would I need to." She stopped talking as a memory flooded her mind. Once when she was about seven, she told her best friend about the ghosts she talked to. Her friend dumped her, and they never played together again. She wanted a friend so badly that when her ghost friend asked to share she just let them. It felt so good to have someone to play with that she didn't realize she was actually seeing with her eyes until it was over. It scared her. She didn't want to tell her mom what happened and never did it again. "Just tell me what to do."

The process took less than a minute and when it was done she gazed at the world with tears in her eyes. The neighborhood was shit but she didn't care. The colors were beautiful, the browns of the building and the gray of the sidewalk. She lifted her new eyes to the sky and marveled at the blues growing dark in the beginning of twilight. Half the stores were boarded up and she couldn't imagine the walkups above them were any better. Garbage was piled against the building and a giant rat scurried from one pile to the next.

Her shadows combined with his eyesight giving her new world a slight overlay. People's auras weren't as clear anymore. One person out of the few she saw had an aura strong enough for her to still see.

In her head, Lance brought his attention back to what they were doing. "We need to hurry, let's go."

She went through the front door and took the stairs to the third floor of the walkup. The walls were covered with graffiti, some of it quite good, but the smell of piss permeated everything. The door was ajar. The guy they followed was in another room making too much noise. They grabbed the iron pole that was used to lock the door and hefted it like an extra-long baseball bat.

When he came through the door, Lance swung for a homerun but Leda still maintained some control of her body and pulled back. It still knocked the wind out of the guy so he couldn't get up right away. "Are you trying to kill him?"

"Yes, he deserves it." He directed her to a drawer by the sink. "Let's get the duct tape. That will hold him until your cop gets here."

"You're using my body and I'll be damned if I let you kill anybody while here. Get over it. Now, how do you know about the duct tape in a drawer?"

"I've crashed here from time to time. Hurry before he gets up."

She/they ran into the next room. Even she did not know what to call them together anymore. Their target was wobbling but standing, and he had a switchblade in his right hand.

"Who the hell are you? You're that blind lady from the alley. How did you find me? Never mind, you won't be alive long enough to tell anybody."

She let Lance lead. The voice that came from her was hers but not. "Now Razor you ain't gonna hurt this lady."

"How do you know that name?"

"Because I gave it to you."

"Lady, I don't even know you, and the guy who gave me that nickname is dead."

"Yes, I am. So why did you do it?"

Razor's hand dropped a couple inches. Leda noticed the change in stance and demeanor. Fear glazed Razor's eyes.

"Bullshit." He said.

"I didn't think you would actually do it, you know? I thought we were partners if not friends. Is that the knife you stabbed me with? I won't let you do it again and you're not getting away with it.

"No, you can't be . . ."

"Really, who else would know about this place?"

Screaming, Razor ran at them, brandishing the blade in a deadly downward arc. She raised her arms, grabbing his forearm and shifting her body, guiding the arc of the blade in the thigh of her assailant.

Lance was yelling inside her head. "What the hell are you doing?"

"Self-defense classes," she said aloud.

Razor was on the floor hugging his leg. His eyes darting at Leda, shouting at her. "You're dead, dead. Go away."

Lance left her body and stood apart. "It's time for me to go." He looked off to the side. "Your cop is here. Come on I'll help you down."

The jolt left her dizzy and she took a few moments to get herself together. "What's your last name?" she asked as they reached the door.

"Turner. Good luck with your cop." Then he was gone.

Leda opened the door and heard Michael calling her name. "Michael, over here." There were more than one pair of footsteps running towards her. "He's upstairs crying about a small stab wound."

"What?" Michael ran upstairs to the room where the guy was yelling.

After Razor was loaded into the car and taken away, Michael came back to where she sat on the stoop. "Leda, what happened? The guy was hysterical, muttering about dead ghosts, like there's any other kind."

"There might be. I'm not discounting anything." She reached out a hand and he placed it on his arm. "Take me home and I'll tell you the whole story on the way. It will be an even more exciting version if we pick up some food on the way. I seem to have missed dinner."

She just finished the story as they stepped into her small efficiency apartment, where everything was in its place. He called the precinct to check on his suspect.

"Well looks like your guy was the lookout for the shooter. He also confessed to a cold case from last year. One Robert Sharp, also known as Razor, was arrested for accessory to murder for the dead white guy and the first degree murder of Lance Turner whose body was found last year. The pocket watch belonged to Lance, one his mother and brother had been looking for. It was given to him by his dead father. "

She smiled sadly. "I guess that's what he was hanging around for. I hope he found peace. And thank you for walking me home. Most people would have dropped me off and run screaming in the other direction."

She led him to her couch, kicked off her shoes and they sat with their bodies turned toward each other.

"What you did back there was amazing, and this has been happening your whole life? Why didn't you try to tell anyone else?"

"Oh I did, when I was younger. It didn't go well. So I stopped trying. There was the fear and whispers and people telling my parents to take me to some type of institution because I saw things that weren't there. As I got older I figured I'd get the same reaction I got from family and friends back home so I kept my mouth shut. I even stopped telling my parents it was still happening. I think my mom knew but she let it go. I grew up and tried to ignore the strange part of my life."

"So why now? And why me?"

"Because I got tired of being silent and you were just

lucky. Plus I liked your aura."

"My aura?"

"Yes. I see what you would call a glow around the living. It kind of gives me a sense about people."

"Do you see them in colors, you know, like red for anger, black for confidence or . . ."

"Yes, somewhat. But it's more of a feeling than actually associating a color with an emotion. The stronger the emotion the harder it is to ignore though I've gotten pretty good at ignoring it. I think I'm going to stop ignoring and find out more about what I can do with it." She reached her hand to the table next to the sofa and felt around for her drink, letting him digest what he'd heard before continuing. "So, are you okay or has this totally messed with your reality?"

Michael took a sip of his drink. "I'm actually working up my nerve to ask you on a date."

J.T. Moore

J.T. Moore writes magic with diversity because everyone deserves to be the main character and if she wants to see more POC protagonists in speculative fiction she's going to have to write them. Her mystic lineage shows itself through the silver streak in her hair. She looks for wonder in the world and knows she can always find it in the pages of a good book. J.T. celebrated the completion of the Ray Bradbury challenge to write 52 Stories in 52 weeks with a loud scream, wine and the conviction that she can pursue her dream. An active member of the League of Utah Writers Speculative Fiction Chapters, find her on Twitter @jtmoore487 and on her website: jtmoorewrites.wordpress.com

Still Frame

by Rhiannon Carswell

his hands tangle in my hair
but not as a lover—
a fist clenches around my strands
his strength exposing my throat
his face a breath from mine
rains spit on my turned cheek
his voice shadowed
by a baby's cry
I cannot move, immobilized by fear
pinned beneath his weight
irrevocably, in that moment,
I know he will kill me
and if not now, when?
I cannot shelter my son
from the grave if I go first
to prepare it
but I cannot move
every chemical in my brain
carries the message
to freeze my muscles
ignore the pain from
his grip on my shoulder
my hair plucked from the root

be still, don't fight back
for this moment
so I might see the next
and it stretches
like taffy pulled between teeth—
in its space
I live lifetimes

Rhiannon Carswell

Rhiannon Carswell is an editor of Salt Flats, an online publication, and writes fiction, poetry, creative nonfiction, and academic scholarship with a little freelance on the side to make things spicy. She lives in Salt Lake City, UT with her son and is a serf to her cat, Azog the Defiler.

Raven the Third

by Talysa Sainz

T he bag over Brigit's head stunk of vomit, sweat, blood, and shame. But despite the smell, she was grateful to hide her face while marching to her death sentence. The light overhead stung her eyes when a guard ripped the bag off her head, taking some of her hair with it.

She frantically looked around. The judging chamber was round, and she was at the center, arms cuffed behind her back, chained to a small metal ring bolted to the stone floor. The room was grimy towards the middle, where she had been pushed to her knees as a prisoner.

Facing her was Chancellor Osvald, the highest authority in Hindarfell other than King Odin himself. The chancellor even outranked the king's son, it was said, even if no one would ever confirm it. He was tall, with strong shoulders, silver hair, and a commanding stance. His callous face reminded her of the cliffsides on the edge of the fjord her parents took her to when she was little—hard and unforgiving, death awaiting with one wrong step.

Flanking the chancellor were two guards: one tall and thin, with short black hair and a scar across his cheek; the other shorter with a thicker build and light brown hair cropped on the sides and long on top.

"Brigit Eskilddotter. You have been accused of attempting to kill your neighbor Sarah."

"I didn't—"

"Silence! Else we will cover your face again."

Brigit never attempted to kill Sarah, but Sarah had turned her in anyway, betting on the hunch that Brigit's heart, thoughts, and memories would betray her. In Hindarfell it was a crime just to want someone dead or to think about killing them. She wanted to keep arguing, but she did not want that horrific bag over her head again. It was hard enough to breathe as it was. She took a deep gulp of air, trying to calm her mind and access any control over herself she might have left.

She was not a murderer.

"You will be judged according to your crimes and sentenced immediately." Chancellor Osvald held out his right hand and looked toward the wall on Brigit's left. A woman came forward, out of the shadow.

Brigit paled. This was one of the Ravens. Looking around the room she saw all three Ravens, one behind her and one on her right, all three with sleek black hair, sharp features, and olive-tinged tawny skin. She knew they were only sixteen, but they looked more like eternal and ageless young women. The first walked up to her and placed her hand on Brigit's head.

An eerie feeling fell over her. Her mind felt cloudy, crowded; she couldn't focus her thoughts or feelings. Memories shot through her mind, one after another. Memories of Viktor, mostly—their time together and the day Viktor's wife, Sarah, confronted her.

"She spent a lot of time with the victim's husband over the last few months. . . . They met often and shared personal stories with each other. . . . The victim confronted her in the middle of town and accused her of having an affair. . . . No affair took place, but she knew there were plenty of rumors about the two of them together."

When the first Raven took her hand off Brigit's head, she winced. Her mind felt sharp, focused once again. She did not like being stripped of that consciousness or having someone else inside her brain. She squirmed, unable to escape the feeling of invasiveness.

Chancellor Osvald nodded at the Raven on his right, who retreated, and gestured to the one in front of him, behind Brigit. The second Raven came forward. Like the first, she put her hand on Brigit's head. This time her mind raced—as if everything she felt and thought in the moment was trying to burst out all at once.

"She does not believe she is a harm to anyone else or that she would or could ever kill someone. But she is afraid of what we might read in her mind. . . . We are all darker than we want to be. . . . She does not want to die."

The chancellor smiled, and it sent her stomach acid into her throat. She knew this man did not care one bit whether she wanted to die or not. She doubted he cared what anyone said in the trial—he had already made up his mind. She was already sentenced. She was already dead.

Another nod and the Raven retreated. Chancellor Osvald beckoned the third Raven forward.

Brigit's stomach turned even more. Everyone knew what powers the Ravens possessed—one could see her memories, one could see her thoughts, and one could see her desires—but she had heard especially harsh words about the third one. She had heard horror stories about how she could read a person's heart, see all their hopes and dreams, and judge them on their desires. She would sentence a life to death for the very things that made them human.

Brigit tried her best to want the right things, to want what was best for Sarah and Viktor. She always planned on doing the right thing, even if she didn't always follow through. She wanted to make a difference, to help people, to feel alive and matter to someone, to anyone. Brigit hung her head. None of that mattered anymore.

The third Raven stepped forward and placed her hand on Brigit's head, lighter than the first two. Her head swirled and she felt foggy, though not quite as much as she did with the first two.

Her heart was on fire. Everything she wanted increased, expanded, burned. Wanting, needing to be thought of as good. Destroying her life over and over until she found one that fulfilled her. She could see herself doing a hundred different things—some wondrous and some horrible—that all filled her desire to matter. The crush on Viktor became all-encompassing. More than ever she wanted Sarah out of his life, to free him from her, but also for herself.

"She seeks affirmation. A status. . . . She wants Viktor in her life, but not Sarah. . . . She does not want to hurt anyone, but . . ." The hands on her head tightened, but it was nothing to the crushing realization of what she truly wanted. "She wishes her neighbor Sarah was dead."

Chancellor Osvald dismissed the third Raven back to the shadow on the right with a wicked smile in his eyes. Brigit avoided his gaze. She was disgusted with herself.

"Brigit Eskilddotter. The evidence speaks for itself.

You are guilty, and I hereby sentence you to death." He motioned to the guards flanking him. "Take her to the dungeon. Her execution will be at first light."

The guards came forward, and put that horrid canvas bag over her head, and hauled her to her feet. Several minutes she walked blind, stumbling, the metal around her wrists cutting through deeper with every jerk of the chain. She almost fell more than once when she followed them down a cold set of stairs and heard a heavy door opening.

The stench that met her next made her glad for the bag covering most of the scent. They must have reached the dungeon. The guards led her to her cell, removed the bag but left the chains, locked her in, and left. No food, no water. For a moment she was grateful she would only be here one night—one small, devastating moment before she remembered that she was dying in the morning.

Dying.

Because she wanted someone dead.

Guilt boiled through her until she vomited in the corner.

She deserved to die. She might as well be guilty of murder if she were the type of person who wanted someone dead. Sarah was an awful, abusive spouse, that Viktor would never leave for his honor and their little girl. But she was breaking him, piece by piece. He deserved better, and she deserved whatever stopped her from hurting him anymore.

Brigit deserved to want her dead. And if that was a crime worthy of death, so be it. If she deserved to die, she would not go out like a coward.

After several hours, a sliver of pale light appeared on the floor of her cell and grew slowly before a shadow crossed over it and the light disappeared. Brigit's heart leapt. Someone must have entered the dungeon.

Viktor. It had to be. Who else in this world would care enough to say goodbye?

Instead, Brigit saw a deep purple and black cloak that matched the dresses worn by the Ravens who had helped sentence her to her death. She retreated as far as she could.

The face of the third Raven, the one who saw inside her heart, appeared in the dim candlelight outside her cell door. She fumbled with a set of keys Brigit was sure she wasn't supposed to have.

"What are you doing?"

"I'm breaking you out of here."

Whatever Brigit was expecting, it wasn't that. Why would this monster break the law she upheld so viciously, and for someone like her?

"Why?"

The Raven stopped. "Why? Because you don't deserve to be here. You don't deserve your sentencing. Don't you want to escape?"

In shock Brigit spouted the words she had rehearsed to herself all night. "I'm guilty. I wanted someone dead. I broke the law."

Confusion crossed the Raven's features. "The law is unfair. You do not deserve to die."

"Then why did you convict me?" Brigit shouted. "If you hadn't told the chancellor what you saw in my head, he wouldn't have known, and I would have gone free." And she wouldn't have been able to live with herself anyway. Not knowing she was a murderer in waiting and unfit for a communal society.

"The chancellor . . . has his ways," the Raven muttered, looking down.

Brigit meant to ask, "What is your name?" but it came out, "Do you have a name?"

The Raven paused. "Darcella," she said.

Brigit had a feeling Darcella wasn't telling the whole truth, but she didn't press it.

"Darcella, I broke the law as it is written. That the law is unfair is your problem. I wanted someone dead, and for that, I am guilty. I will take my punishment." Saying the words aloud only firmed her desires. She abhorred the cruelty she harbored in her heart and longed to extinguish it. Her village was not safe with the potentially dangerous.

"You have the chance to take a stand. Do not waste it. You cannot stand for anything without your life."

Never would Brigit have been able to predict standing in a prison, arguing with her judge for her death sentence. Maybe she couldn't see into the future like this—witch, seer, goddess, monster, whatever she was—could, but she knew she couldn't live with herself after being condemned by her own heart. "And what do you stand for?"

Loud steps outside the door told her guards in their armor were coming down the stairs. They must have heard her yelling. Time was running out. If they found a Raven here trying to help her escape, it would be her fault—her heart that condemned another.

Darcella still didn't answer her. Brigit's core filled with sympathy. She didn't see a monster. She didn't see a god. She saw a scared teenage girl who was just as trapped as she was. A girl who wanted desperately to do what was right but had to follow the law.

Brigit shook her head. This girl's guilt was not on her

conscience. Brigit knew her wrongdoing, but she was good, and she would take her punishment. No more, no less.

But Darcella was not waiting. She pulled on Brigit's arm and said, "Die on your own time. Die by your choice, but I am getting you out of here."

"This is my choice!" Brigit grabbed Darcella's hands and put them on her head. Immediately her head swirled once more, but this time she knew what to expect. She focused on what she really wanted—to take her punishment, to make her statement with her death, to die instead of live knowing what crimes she was capable of.

As Brigit dropped her hands, Darcella did as well. She backed away, tears streaming down her eyes.

Guards' voices came closer. Darcella looked at the door and back at Brigit with panic in her face. If they walked in now, they would know the Raven had tried to break her out, and Brigit would die as a coward as well. Brigit pushed her out of the cell completely and shut the door.

"Lock the door," she ordered.

Darcella complied and hid the keys in her dress, just soon enough for guards to run in, see her at the cell, and seize her. After escorting her from the dungeon, Chancellor Osvald walked in. His nose squished up, obviously disgusted by the stench.

He stood before Brigit's cell and pulled on the door, which wouldn't move.

"Looks like we had a near escape on our hands."

"Actually, no, you didn't." She didn't worry about sounding respectful. There was nothing more he could do to her now.

He narrowed his eyes down at her, and Brigit was shocked to find belief in his face, mixed in with the disgust.

"Even so. We can't risk this happening again. Prisoners will now be executed immediately after sentencing."

Brigit felt hollow. She couldn't summon a tear for herself or for anyone else's future.

The chancellor whistled and the same two guards from her trial came forward, one carrying the keys he had taken from the third Raven moments before. Shorty opened the cell and fastened her hands behind her back once more. The other brought forward the same filthy canvas bag, and she almost lost her resolve to go quietly. Yet she didn't struggle when they put the bag of stench and shame over her head for the last time.

They led her on a short walk, up the stairs, around the corner, long stretch, heavy door, brisk night air, across a field, up wooden steps, onto a platform. She felt a thick rope around her neck, tighter, tighter.

Her sentencing was read, the chancellor's smug voice being the last one she heard. She focused on the crickets playing their symphony in the night. Not only would her death be quick and ignominious, but inconsequential. No public execution. No one to say goodbye. The earth itself couldn't see her face as she said farewell and fell through the scaffold.

Talysa Sainz

Talysa Sainz is a freelance editor who believes life's deepest truths can be found in fiction. She runs her own editing business and spends her time at the library or volunteering with the League of Utah Writers. Always fascinated with the structure of words, she studied English Linguistics and Editing at BYU. She then went on to receive a Master of Science in Management and Leadership. Talysa is the President of the Utah Freelance Editors.

Time Machines Only Go One Way

by John M. Olsen

The symposium on time travel was a total waste of time, except for Doctor Eigen Grolier's presentation. I'd skipped my lunch break to attend this session after it caught my eye. I listened intently, being one of only three attendees to hear the man's wild ramblings on spatial membranes, reference frames, neural rewiring, and what he called "the mistake of mislabeling dark matter." Unlike all the other speakers, I couldn't immediately discredit his ideas.

He closed his presentation with a startling claim. "It works. I've actually done it. I skipped forward in time." It was a bold claim, and one I could put some work into debunking, based on my copious notes. He looked the part of a mad scientist with his wild, uncombed hair pulled back into a rough ponytail. His short beard looked more like he'd lost his razor weeks ago.

The other attendees wandered off, noses glued to their phone screens. I intercepted Doctor Grolier at the stairs of the small stage. "That's quite an accomplishment, to travel in time."

He waved a dismissive hand. "You don't believe me. Nobody does. It's made a mess of my life. My wife first thought I'd run off when I vanished for a year, but then she had me declared dead before I reappeared. I need to reverse the process and fix everything."

"Reverse it? You believe that's possible? I've heard there are problems with causality."

"Yes, but bifurcating realities addresses that. I only need one reality where I've returned to my origin time. This universe can do whatever it wants."

"What lab are you working out of?" If I could visit and see what he was doing, it would be simpler to declare it all a scam. Some said I took odd scientific claims too personally, like I was on a crusade to rid the world of false hopes. Maybe they were right.

"I have no lab. I lost my job and access to equipment because I didn't request a sabbatical. Chaos and ruin."

No lab. Nothing to verify. The odds of him being a total crackpot rose. "If you have already traveled through time, why can't you go back?" As long as I was digging for info, I might as well get a few more details on the weak spots in his story.

"The initial process only goes one way. I have to rewrite my theories to reverse everything so I can go back in time the way I skipped forward. Now, if you will excuse me, I'm pressed for time, as it were." He chuckled at his joke as he sidestepped me and strode out the door.

I passed the podium and saw a lone sheet of paper left behind. With a quick look, I realized it contained notes and equations he'd not discussed in his presentation, along with an illustration of a wire globe. I grabbed it and ran to the hall and looked both ways, but he was gone, lost in the crowd as the neighboring auditoriums emptied.

With his equations and designs, I could quickly disprove him and write him off as delusional, or decide if he deserved more of my attention. I hurried back to my apartment, enjoying the early afternoon spring weather along the way.

With my desk cleared, I set out a new notepad and fired up the computer. The equations weren't hard to understand, but the connections between them seemed incomplete, tenuous at best. Some seemed unrelated and irrelevant. I'd scribbled my way through half the pages of my notepad when my phone chimed with Christie's ringtone. I picked up.

"Weren't you going to join us for dinner?"

Was it that time already? I glanced at the clock to see it was past seven. I was late for our date with friends. "Sorry, I was distracted and lost track of time."

"I'll order for you."

"Thanks. I've got one quick thing I'd like to work out before I join you. I'll be there in a few minutes."

Someone knocked at the door. It was dark outside. How had it become nine o'clock? I stumbled to the door to find an angry Christie holding a bag with a restaurant logo. "Here's your food."

I caught the bag as she dropped it.

"I'm sorry."

"I know. You lost track of time again. We had fun. Misty and Jake are planning a trip to Florida over the break. They want a little together time before the baby arrives. They make the most adorable couple."

The familiar conversation ate at me, always the same. I got distracted by my work and lost track of time, and she suffered for it. No matter the social event, I failed to show up more than I succeeded. Here I was, hurting the love of my life, and at a loss for what more I could say. It crushed me to disappoint her. I'd done it too many times.

Her choppy summary, and the hints about being a couple, confirmed I was in deep trouble. It would take superhuman efforts to overcome. I had to dedicate some time to her, to do something together. "Let me make it up to you. I'll be done teaching at three tomorrow. Want to come over after that? I'm building something new."

She shook her head in dismay. "One of these days I need to teach you how to invite a girl over in a way that actually sounds fun. Then I'll make you promise to only use your newfound crafty wiles on me, and none of the other girls." She let out a weak laugh. At least she could find humor in the problem I'd caused. "I'll come over tomorrow afternoon. While you show me your new toys, I have some new ideas I'd like to bounce off you for my thesis. My advisor says the conclusion is weak, and you're great at spotting and fixing gaps in logic." She lingered for a moment before leaving me with a brief kiss and a wave goodbye.

I set the food to the side of my desk. Tomorrow, I would make things better with Christie and put us back on the right foot. Enticed by the aromas of alfredo sauce and fresh bread, I grabbed a roll and glanced back over the equations left by Doctor Grolier. The equations would take effort to memorize, but I'd found long ago that memorization helped me to find connections between what looked like unrelated data.

The waveform mathematics played against a wire network built into a sphere large enough to crawl into, almost like a faraday cage. Instead of blocking all electrical signals, it was meant to focus and redirect specific frequencies internally.

Thoughts created memories by forming specific neural pathways. Those connective paths inside my head then led to the next step, and the next, as I pondered the mathematical relationships. The stepwise learning process was more than memorizing information. It was a construction project on a cellular scale, rewiring the neural links within my brain. All learning built neural paths. That was the basis behind memories, but this felt different.

The wire mesh illustration on the paper wasn't quite right, so I corrected it. What had told me it was wrong? I pulled out a spool of electrical wire and a soldering gun and set to work with the math still running through my head, building and refining neural paths and memories like electronic circuitry.

Sunlight poured in through the window. How long had the sun been up? By the angle, it was well past noon. The complete soldered wire mesh stood around me as I sat cross-legged inside. A now-cold soldering iron lay on the floor beside me. Glancing at my notes, I'd misunderstood the relationships between equations. My thoughts had been shallow and limited before. I was closer than ever to understanding it all. A sense of purpose and direction filled me; A burning need to complete what I'd begun and see it through to the end. Something powerful sat just out of reach, if only I could take one more step into the dark.

It came to me that the wire mesh redirected and reflected brain waves. Holding certain thought patterns allowed me to reprogram additional neural paths. Like software loaded into a computer, I could now analyze the structure of time as never before. Elation built at the thought of my success so far, but a piece was missing. If I pushed a little harder, I could touch the connections that held me to my frame of reference. I not only felt the connections, but I could also control and manipulate them. I could move my little bubble universe forward with a thought, but how far? A day? A year? What about a century? Millenia were within my grasp. All I had to do was . . .

A knock sounded at my apartment door, then it changed to pounding. Finally, the door flew open. Christie came in and gasped when she saw me sitting on the floor inside my wire thought amplifier.

The amplified signal grew in my mind and fought against my thoughts of Christie, generating dissonance. Logic and emotions clashed. Before me sat two perpendicular paths intersecting at one point. I had to choose which path to follow. In one direction lay proof, and in the other, love.

My vision flashed, and I backed off the mental pressure in an instant. The room became dark with a street light shining through the window. It was dark, but not silent. Shuddering breaths reached me.

Christie sat on my couch curled into a ball, rocking back and forth as she clutched my favorite sweatshirt, the one she had given to me for my birthday.

"I'm here, Christie."

She gasped and sat up, reaching to turn on a table lamp beside the couch, nearly knocking it over. "They said you never showed up to teach today. I came over and thought I saw you, but you vanished. You and that wire cage."

The cage. My amplifier. It still gave my thoughts focus. I had skipped forward only a few hours. The power to jump forward still flowed through me, with the ability to prove myself a success. I hesitated as I took in her grief. I had caused her pain. Not just this once, but never so badly as this. She deserved more from me, and better.

Christie stumbled across the room and reached through the wires to touch my cheek, sending a flash of static electricity between us. I twitched at the shock.

The equations dropped from my thoughts like a brick dropping through sheets of glass. My hands regained feeling I hadn't realized I'd lost. I reached out and grabbed the wire mesh around me, bending and distorting it with my clumsy grasp. The mental images remained, but without the external support of the wire shell, my thoughts lost their power.

Christie stood straighter, glanced at the uneaten food still sitting beside my desk, then back at me. "What happened? You look like death warmed over. Talk to me, or I'm dragging you to the hospital right now." She lifted the bent wire framework and tossed it aside in a heap. She patted a hand against my cheek, harder than strictly necessary. "Say something." Her voice quavered.

I saw Christie's worried face, and my heart lurched. I'd nearly lost her—the most important thing in my life—without realizing it. "I've missed opportunities for months. I've failed you and our friends over and over. Now, this nearly ruined it all." I waved at the crumpled wire.

My time travel project had forced my poorly placed focus to the foreground. The siren call of what I could do had overwhelmed what I should do. Behind all this stood a new clarity of thought, something Doctor Grolier had missed in his rush for success at all costs. Grolier had discovered too late that ignoring the costs and grasping at a partial solution led to failure.

"The poor fool. He was right that time machines only go one way, but he was wrong to think he could control the direction. Time machines only go forward. There is no bifurcation of the universe." I took Christie's hand in mine with an apologetic smile.

"Okay, I admit those were words. Now say something that makes sense, or I still take you to the hospital." She sniffed and wiped at her eyes with her free hand.

"I love you."

It was up to me to live in the now. To be part of the present. To act. To participate. To be the one to make a difference every day. I wanted to share my time with Christie rather than merely exist in isolation with my ideas and projects. It was pointless to skip forward through time with no impact on the world around me. My heart told me to teach a new generation of young minds to love not just science, but life. Nobody could live my life but me, and it was to be lived here and now.

I tossed Doctor Grolier's page of notes and my over-flowing notebook into the trash, then hugged Christie and spun her in a circle, breathing in the faint lilac scent of her hair. Relief filled me. I hadn't lost her, and her intervention had saved me from myself.

John M. Olsen

John M. Olsen edits and writes speculative fiction across multiple genres and loves stories about ordinary people stepping up to do extraordinary things. He encourages other writers at every opportunity and hopes to see the local community produce many more great authors. He loves to create and fix things, whether editing or writing novels or short stories or working in his secret lair equipped with dangerous power tools. In all cases, he applies engineering principles and processes to the task at hand, often in unpredictable ways.

He lives in Utah with his lovely wife and a variable number of mostly grown children and a constantly changing subset of extended family.

Monochromatic

by Danielle Harward

D ear Lily,
    I want to tell you what happened. I need to explain. This week . . . it didn't go at all how I expected. Or how I wanted.

But things don't always turn out how we want.

It started when I got home from my business trip to Italy. Mr. Peterson had sprung it on me. The plane barely touched down before I got the call from him. He wanted me to come into the office. Now. I thought I had done something wrong. His tone wasn't happy, but it never was. It's something I think would annoy you about him.

Once I got there, I sat in the hard leather seats across from his desk. His office, made up of various shades of gray, told me his decor was probably a wide range of colors I couldn't yet see. I wondered how I would view his office once we got married.

He pinned me with a stern look and then asked me a question I truly wasn't prepared for.

Why should I get the partner position?

It confused me. It seemed like a silly question. I had proved myself again and again over the past seven years. I rose higher in this company when others chose to leave. I put my best foot forward. But Mr. Peterson wasn't a patient man, so my answer had to come quickly.

I told him I should get the position because I deserved it.

He snorted and countered that everyone in the running for the job deserved it. "So, why should you be the one to get it? How different are you from them?" He didn't like repeating himself. I could tell I had annoyed him. Strike one.

My mind raced. All I could think about was you. I wanted to tell him I had found my soulmate and this job would allow me to be everything you needed. Visions of us together as a family pounded in my head as I fought for an answer. But I knew Mr. Peterson needed something more. He wasn't the sentimental type.

A minute flashed by. I was taking too long to answer. Strike two. He frowned at me now. His fingers drummed on the arm of his chair. My throat was so tight. Finally, I blurted the first thing which came to mind that wasn't you.

"I could get you into the golf club you like for free."

I thought he might smack me. I wanted to smack me. What a stupid useless thing to say. You would have laughed if you had been there.

Mr. Peterson stared at me as I struggled not to squirm under his ire. Nightmares of him firing me right then and there flashed before my eyes. I was so worried I had ruined my chance of being with you. I wanted to vomit.

But then, he smiled. And his smile turned into a laugh which billowed through his office. I chuckled along with him nervously until he finally gained control of himself. He told me I would do just fine and congratulations. I would start my new position as partner first thing on Monday. I could have screamed! I was so excited.

Monochromatic

But all I really wanted to do was tell you.

You, sweet Lily, changed my life in so many ways.

The dress you wore was such a rich exquisite color the first time I saw you it surprised me. It was a fall day. A cool breeze tickled my arm, and it toyed with your dress as you walked. I still remember the smell of the food vendors all over the market. Fried chicken, hamburgers, and fries in all their greasy glory. In my hand, I held an ice cream, cold, sticky liquid dripped onto my fingers. My world of gray and white had a bright spot in it. I perceived colors that weren't the usual gray tones. The contrast between you and the rest of the world was so strong I blinked my eyes several times. I thought something was wrong until I realized what you were. My other half. My soulmate.

They told us what it would be like to lay eyes on our soulmates in school. Many had tried to describe to us what it was like the first time your eyes perceived color. Our world in its entirety would be awash with color the day we married our soulmate. I had always wished it would happen, but at the same time, I doubted it would happen to me. Some people never found their soulmates. I always assumed I would be one of them. Yet there you were: the one person in the world meant to complete me.

You took my breath away.

You walked through the street market. Your curls bounced. Quickly, I stepped behind a building and peered around the corner. I remember hearing my heartbeat in my chest. I couldn't believe your beauty. As you walked from vendor to vendor picking fruits and vegetables, you gave them each a gentle smile. Jewelry gleamed at your ears and wrists. Bright metal to match the belt around your slim waist. My fingers clutched the corner bricks. I wanted to rush to you and show you I was your soulmate. Me.

But then I looked down at myself. I wore dirty jeans and a stained shirt ice cream cone halfway melted onto my hand. In that instance, I realized I wasn't good enough for you. How could I be? I had no money. I was fresh out of college, living in my childhood bedroom. What would you think if I introduced you to my parents and told you I lived with them in the same sentence? You were a divine goddess. I knew you would hate me as your soulmate with how I was. I didn't deserve you. Would you know it too?

I ripped my gaze away from you and pressed my back against the warm brick wall as I formed a plan. I wanted to be with you, I ached for it. Maybe I could be good enough for you? Maybe I could become enough. I tossed the nearly melted ice cream into a trashcan as my thoughts raced. I needed to get my life together for you. Then, we could meet. We could be genuinely happy together.

I followed far behind you as my plan solidified. How long would it take me to be worthy of you? I knew it would be a few years at least. But it would be worth it. I could see our happiness together solidifying into something truly amazing. I could see myself becoming the man you deserved. Sliding your key into a door, you disappeared into an apartment complex.

Knowing where you lived, I raced home. I knew my father would help me. He'd been droning on about me getting a "worthwhile" job. The words flew from my mouth like a waterfall as I told him and my mother. My father immediately went to make some calls.

A few days later my mother and I sat together on the

couch. She squeezed my hand. "Henry," she murmured. "She'll love you no matter what, darling. Introduce yourself to her. Don't wait a single moment."

I seriously doubted it.

But my mother pushed. "Not everyone finds their soulmate. When you do, it's a blessing. Take a leap of faith, my son."

I kissed her cheek. "Maybe, Mom," I acknowledged, "but I need to at least be able to provide for her."

"Damn straight," my father agreed as he entered the room and announced he had found me a position in an accounting firm.

I remember getting dressed up in my first suit. It was a hand-me-down from my father and was a little small on me, but it was better than anything the secondhand store had to offer. It was uncomfortable and different from my usual casual dress. But I had taken a few college courses in accounting and was fairly confident I could handle what this job threw at me. I'm a quick learner, but this place was almost too nice for me. As if I were a seagull among hawks. Thinking of you helped. You were my motivation.

So, when I started, I started at a run. Two years raced by with ten-hour days, sometimes more. I rarely saw you. I tried to check in once a month, carefully making sure you didn't see me. Then I'd get home from my horribly long day to force myself to work out.

I started eating differently too. Do you know how frustrating it is to calorie count? It's a terrible way to live. I settled for eating healthier instead. Sometimes, I wasn't strong. But I'd always try again. I wanted to be healthy for you.

Healthy and successful. That picture was like a shot of adrenalin.

My parents are soulmates. I grew up with stories of how they first met each other. They fit together unquestionably, and they knew it in an instant this person was their person. In school, they told us tales of crushingly beautiful ways soulmates met. It was revered. The moment you met your other half and you saw color for the first time was supposed to be a cherished one. Fashion magazines paraded the beauty of Hollywood chance meetings. Newspapers touted people who traveled across the world to find their special someone. It needed to be perfect.

When I had chances to see you, I savored the moments and held them close to my heart. I loved seeing you shine. You wore the most exquisite colors and seeing you brighten the darkness around me made my chest fill with warmth. You left me smiling for days.

Life continued on this way for a few years.

My mom pushed me, asking when I would introduce myself.

"My son," she would say with worry creasing her brow, "This determination to change yourself so you may be good enough for her is unhealthy. Please, just introduce yourself to her. I promise she will love you as you are." I would smile and brush off her comments. She hadn't seen you yet. She didn't know how wonderful you were, how much you deserved.

I achieved the health I wanted but hadn't gained the income. I was barely scraping by, and I wanted to be sure I could take care of your every need. My Dad assured me if I kept my nose to the grind, a promotion would come.

He was right.

After four years of watching young, tired men finally give up on the firm, Mr. Peterson called me into his office.

An opportunity came up since the department manager was retiring, and he wanted to offer me the job. It wasn't a lot more money than I was already making, but it was enough for me to start saving for a house. I took the job so fast Mr. Peterson wasn't done detailing it before I said yes.

My plan was to work hard, save enough for a down payment on a house, and have some extra on the side for a beautiful wedding. I'd imagine you would like an extravagant wedding with lots of color. And now, I had more time to see you. With regular hours set at this position, I had the chance to learn your schedule. I found you were an architect, a fact which pleased me more than I expected. Beautiful and smart. You were the whole package. It looked like you worked with a small group of people on the third floor of an office building close enough for you to walk to. You liked yoga too. Sometimes, you would go to a small Zen place on Saturdays with your yoga mat.

But most of all, each and every time I saw you, you always caused me butterflies.

You seemed successful. I regularly saw you walking home with rolls of plans under one arm and your purse hanging from the other. You often visited the doctor in those years. Once a month, in fact. I was proud you cared so much about your physical health. I had become a bit of a health nut myself. We had something in common already.

The market remained a favorite of yours. And in turn mine. You went almost every Sunday. I decided I should learn to cook the foods you like in my spare time. Turns out, not only do I like cooking, but I'm fairly good at it. A lot like accounting, food has its own language. The secrets of the sizzle tell you the precise moment it's ready. Plus, when the time was right, I wanted to make your favorite foods for you.

Three more years passed. I almost had enough for a down payment, and Mr. Peterson was putting me through the wringer at work without a word of admiration. He wanted me to become a partner of the firm. I wanted it too. I had my eye on a gorgeous house I thought you would love. It had some common themes you used in your architectural designs. I've studied the finished results of your projects. Turns out, you've designed many buildings here, including a library downtown. Your work is exemplary. I could tell by each careful detail you put your heart into each building. But to get the house, I needed to be a partner.

Then it would be time.

The day I left for Italy I remember knocking on Mr. Peterson's door gently, hoping the voice telling me to come in would be happy and not a gruff. It seemed I had pulled the short end of the stick because my answer to come in was curt.

Once again, the hard leather seats held me as he organized the papers on his desk into a clean stack, clicking them against the desk. I waited. You learn a thing or two about someone when you work for them for seven years. I knew he didn't like wasting time on small talk or reassurances.

"I need you to go to Italy," he said.

My eyebrows shot so high they must have disappeared into my hairline. The firm had clients everywhere, but Italy? I'd never been there before. Or so far away from you.

"For how long?" I asked. A careful question.

He narrowed his eyes at me. I could hear his words before he said them. "Wrong question. You should be asking me about the customer you're going to meet."

Right. He was right. But Lily, I was worried about leaving you for so long. I nodded, and he continued to tell me about an offshores investment group I would be helping. He wanted me there for five weeks. I wanted to say no. So badly, I wanted to say no. I could feel the small word sitting behind my lips, waiting to be spoken. Mr. Peterson sensed my hesitation and didn't like it.

"You can go to Italy, or you can walk away from the partner position," he warned.

So, I went to Italy.

I wished I could have seen it with you first. Even in monochrome, it's a breathtaking place. My days were engulfed with the work I was doing but my nights were entirely my own. For dinners, I ate pasta in warm, bright restaurants with live music. I walked the streets and passed many lovers hand in hand. I often found myself daydreaming about taking you there. What would it be like to see you light up as you took in the Colosseum? What would you think of the fountains splashing or the small market carts offering rustic Italian specialties?

I was so close to being ready for you. The hope of it warmed my chest like wildfire. Those five weeks felt like an eternity. All I wanted was to see your face.

Now, I've arrived at where we started, returning home from Italy and finally getting the position I needed.

As soon as I stepped out of Mr. Peterson's office, I called my realtor and had him set up a walkthrough tomorrow. I could not wait to show you.

Everything was perfect. So, I began heading your way.

I have to admit, it was a little surprising you had never moved this entire time. But it was okay because it showed me you didn't mind staying somewhere for a long time. I picked up some flowers on the way. I asked the vendor for the brightest ones he had. I think you'd like the colors. They smelled like spring.

When I walked along the sidewalk, my stomach turned. I now wore a well-fitted pinstripe suit with shiny black leather shoes. I tripped twice before I forced my feet to walk more carefully. My legs were jelly. I was your soul-mate, we were biologically meant for each other, but I was still so nervous. Was I good enough for you? Would you still find me lacking in some way? At the steps of your building, I paused, clearing my mind and taking a deep breath. This was a moment I wanted to remember for a long time. I willed my racing heartbeat to steady itself before I ascended the stairs.

After I turned the corner to your apartment I'm not sure how my feet moved forward anymore. I clenched the flowers to stop my hands from shaking. It was like an out-of-body experience. I got to your door, held up my flow-ers, and knocked twice, offering my warmest smile.

Silence waited on the other side of the door.

You shouldn't be at work today. But maybe you were out? I had passed the market on the way in, and I didn't see you. I knew you didn't usually do yoga on the week-ends. I also hadn't seen you with any friends besides your coworkers. I told myself it was fine and tried to slow the rapid thumping in my chest.

You probably just didn't hear me. I had seen you walking around with earbuds on. I knocked louder. Three times.

Still nothing.

My palms began to sweat as ragged breaths rushed in and out of my lungs.

The door to the right of yours opened, and a young woman peered out at me, confused. She asked if I knew you. It was a question I couldn't say yes or no to, so I asked if you were out instead.

Her eyes widened as she whispered, "I'm so sorry dear, but no, she died."

With those words, my heart broke.

She went on to tell me your thin body wasn't because you took care of it. It was because of cancer. Your doctor appointments were for radiation. But after fighting it for seven years, you couldn't fight any longer.

I asked your neighbor so many questions, and she answered them all. You kept a job only because you needed to pay the bills. You distanced yourself from most people because you knew you were dying. You didn't make any big purchases, hence why you didn't have a car or a house. The neighbor never saw or heard you talk about your family. She even admitted she might have been the person you were closest to outside of work.

You were alone in the end.

Now, I'm sitting on the graveyard bench, a few feet away from your headstone. All the years I could have had with you are gone.

We will never meet and fill each other's world with color. What kind of soulmate leaves the other alone to die? Perhaps I deserve the dull existence I will now live without you in my life. I don't know how to move on. I don't know what to do. I am lost. I feel as if my chest is empty. Do I even have a heartbeat anymore? All is forever gray.

Always yours,
Henry

Danielle Harward

Danielle Harward is a high fantasy author who enjoys spinning tales full of heroes and magic. Her work explores the difficulty of conquering inner conflict and the line between good and villainous themes. As a full time employee and mother, Danielle finds time to write in the wee hours of the night or at the crack of dawn — depending on how exhausted she is by the end of the day. But juggling writing, family, and work is worth it for her because she has wanted to be a writer since she was eight years old and began reading her first fantasy novel.

She holds an Associates degree in Business Management from Snow College and is a member of The League of Utah Writers. She has published several news articles with The Chronicle Progress, a short story through The League of Utah Writers 85th Anthology, and a short story through Camden Press's Street Magic Anthology.

Contact Danielle by email at: Harward.danielle@yahoo.com

Intertwined

by Holly Voss

*M*x. *and Mrs. Cam and Tracy Lin*
  Cam traces their finger over the embossed letters. They make everything real the way the $2,000 deposit on the banquet hall hadn't. Cam had known this was where Tracy's proposal had been leading, and not for the first time they can feel the weight of the promises they've made measured against the ones they're about to make anew.

Tracy's tiny arms wrap around Cam's waist. "Are you over here angsting again, babe?"

"Hardly," Cam lies. Tracy sighs, and Cam knows they've been caught. Tracy's always been able to see right through them. Cam turns in Tracy's arms and drapes their own over her shoulders. "Just making sure everything's ready to go over here."

Tracy raises a perfectly trimmed eyebrow but accepts the small truth as the concession it is and doesn't push. "Well, the caterer is ready to go, and the rabbi is just finishing her setup."

"You know you didn't have to—"

Tracy kisses the words from Cam's lips. "You're taking my name, and we both know your religion has always meant more to you than mine ever has. I promise, this is just the way I wanted it to go."

Cam chases the promise on their wife-to-be's lips. They're not sure if they believe her, but she hasn't lied to them yet.

"Now, come on. It's high time we both got dressed for this little shindig."

"Is that what we're calling this?" Cam asks, gesturing at the banquet hall. The white and blue flowers filling the room only serve to reinforce how far Tracy's willing to go to accommodate them. "A little shindig?"

Tracy shakes her head, but it doesn't hide her smile. She steps away, gently tugging Cam toward the door. "If that makes it easier for you to handle, then yes."

Cam stops short and pulls Tracy close, resting their forehead against hers. They can feel her eyes on them, but for the moment, all they can focus on is the touch of her skin against theirs.

Tracy reaches one golden hand up to cup the back of Cam's neck. "I'm right here."

Cam inhales, the breath trembling its way through their lungs. "I know."

"I trust you."

Cam hates that she knows what they're scared of. "How can you be so sure about me?"

"Because I know you."

"You think he didn't? That he wasn't sure about me too?"

"I think your former fiancé was sure about the person he thought you were. He was sure about the version of you that was soft-spoken and cautious. The one that played the game and stayed in their place. He was ready to walk down the aisle with that person."

Tracy pulls away, taking Cam's hand and tugging them to the window. The chuppah is in full view from there, the altar shaded by the sheer white cloth draped between the four bamboo poles, and the exterior decked out with carefully strung lilies in white and yellow. Cam's eyes sting. Tracy hadn't asked questions or tried to barter for concessions when Cam had asked about having a Jewish ceremony. She said she'd assumed that was the plan.

Cam doesn't know what they did to deserve her.

Tracy wraps her arms around Cam's waist from behind them and tucks her chin over their shoulder. "He didn't know this you, the one that is brilliant and witty and strong. The one that spent three decades hiding behind what they thought the world wanted from them. The one that wore oversized hoodies all through high school because nothing else fit their chest right. The one that would eat nothing but soup from a can if I let them. That's the you that I fell in love with. That's the you that I'm marrying."

Cam rests their hands on Tracy's wrists at her waist. "You're sure?"

"I'm sure about you, Cam Roshal. Are you sure about me?"

Tracy's conviction releases the tension in Cam's chest. They relax and lean back against her. "I'm sure that I'm not going to be Cam Roshal much longer."

There's a smile in Tracy's voice when she speaks. "Good. Then I'll see you in three hours."

After that, the most memorable part of getting ready for the ceremony is the way Darren, Cam's best man, sasses them the whole time. He's always been the wittier of the two of them, and he'd been the first to tell them to leave their now ex-fiancé. It's easy to fall into laughter with him, easy to let him fix their tie when they fumble it. The suit is beautiful, just the right shade of blue to set off their bronze skin. It's not the bright red that Darren would have had them in, but that would have raised more eyebrows in the Lin family than Cam was strictly ready for.

The ceremony is a blur of Tracy's eyes on theirs and both of them fumbling through their processional, through the sheva brachot and their vows. It's an odd collection of what makes Cam who they are and Tracy who she is. The perfect blend of their future together.

Then it's the yichud, and the brief respite it offers from the stress of the last few months. Tracy leads the way back to the bridal suite, and Cam shuts the door behind them once they're inside. They settle on the couch together, taking full advantage of these few, quiet minutes alone before they go back outside to fully celebrate with their friends and family. Cam sinks into Tracy's arms and cries the tears they hadn't let themself cry when she'd proposed. It's real now. They're married, and no one can take that away from them.

Tracy kisses Cam's temple as she runs her fingers through their hair. "Tell me what you're thinking," she says.

Cam leans into Tracy's hand, taking comfort from her touch. "This whole thing has had me scared half to death for months. I figured it would be that way for a while. Feelings that big don't just go away."

"I know."

Cam pulls away and looks Tracy in the eye. "Do you? I thought— I'd hoped that this would all just go away when I saw you there, when you kissed me at the altar, but it didn't. I'm still terrified that I'm going to mess this up."

"Of course you are." Tracy's voice is gentle as she reaches out to run her fingers through Cam's hair again. "That's who you are."

"What's that supposed to mean?"

"It means that I know you. I know you're going to worry about this, about us. And it's my job to remind you that we chose this. Not you, not me, us. Loving you is a choice, Cam, and what we did today is me promising to make that choice every day for the rest of our lives."

The lump in Cam's throat could undo them if they let it. Instead, they swallow past it and lean forward to press their forehead against Tracy's. "Thank you."

"For what?"

"For seeing me." They lean forward and kiss Tracy, tasting her smile. "I'm so lucky to have you."

Tracy laughs, and it's that high, bright laugh that comes when she's feeling free of all the weight and pressure of the world. "Now I know the ceremony's gone to your head, because I'm pretty sure I'm the lucky one in this relationship."

"Trace—"

"You're brilliant, you're kind, and you're the best Pictionary partner a gal could ask for." She kisses Cam's temple again, and this time her lips linger. "If anything, I should be thanking you."

"For what?"

"For being mine."

The moment dangles between them, like the tiny sapphire pendant that Tracy had given them on their first anniversary, threaded through a chain so fine that it was a wonder the pendant didn't fall right through. Tracy's waiting for something—a response, no doubt—and though Cam would have thought themself ill-prepared for such a moment, they have exactly the right words ready and waiting.

Cam cups the back of Tracy's neck and turns so they can face her, their foreheads resting together. "I am. Never doubt."

Tracy smiles against Cam's lips, and time stops meaning much of anything anymore in the safety and seclusion of the room.

Darren bangs on the door three minutes later, just before things get too heated. Cam's grateful that they're not the only one being subjected to Darren's leers. Cam grins at Tracy's blush, kissing the corner of her eye. She still remembers the moment they'd known Tracy was a keeper: when she'd gone shot for shot with Darren and still had enough snark to match him. Even now, though, Darren still gets the drop on her when she's sober.

Darren drags them to the banquet hall, where they're welcomed with cheers and shouts for a kiss. Tracy laughs and pulls Cam into a kiss instantly, ignoring the way Cam's skin goes warm under her hands. They let her pull them toward the head table, their parents on either side. Cam loses track of how many times their friends and family call on them to kiss throughout the meal, but they don't really mind. Any excuse to kiss the love of their life is a good one.

And then it's time for the first dance. It was one of the few things that Tracy had insisted on, and Cam had been more than happy to oblige. But now that the time has come, all Cam can think about is the chance that they might mess this up for her.

Tracy takes Cam's hand in her own and rests the other at their hip. Cam tunes into her instinctively, meeting her eyes and ready to go.

"Trust me."

Cam does.

It's a hell of a thing, being led by Tracy in all her petite ferocity, especially when Cam towers over her even without heels. Cam had tried leading, and that had lasted all of five minutes before both Tracy and their dance coach had tossed that idea out the window. Not that Cam minded. Tracy was the light and fire of their relationship, and if they were going to show the world that, this was the moment to do so.

Cam follows, and Tracy leads, and for those few, blessed moments, nothing matters except the two of them and the way their bodies move together. Tracy makes it all seem effortless, and Cam would envy her if they didn't know exactly how much sweat and tears went into making this look as easy as it does. Twice around the room, a dip, a spin, and now Cam's leading for those few brief moments it takes to lift Tracy into the air so she can fly.

Even if this dance had once been about showing the world who they are, it's become so much more now. It's for them, for their future, for the lives they get to live together, through the joy and the anger and the laughter and the hurt. All of that is here, in this single moment, with Tracy above them and her eyes on theirs, like nothing else in the world matters.

It's perfect.

Cam lowers her to the ground, and it doesn't stop being perfect. They lead through the last circuit around the dance floor, through one last dip, and then it's done. But as they hold her in their arms, feeling the way her chest heaves beneath them, they know that this is only one of many moments. It's special, yes, something to cherish, but it's just the beginning.

"Hey," Tracy says, tugging on Cam's hair. "What's going on in that head of yours?"

"Nothing." Cam lifts Tracy from the dip they'd been holding her in and sets her back on her feet. "Just thinking about how much I love you."

Tracy smacks their shoulder, but they can see the way her skin goes a shade darker. "You're being sappy. It's not like you."

"Maybe not. But am I not allowed to be sappy on the day I married the best woman in the world?"

"Well, I suppose I can give you a free pass, just this once."

"How kind of you."

"Remember that the next time I leave the milk out in the morning."

As Darren intercedes, pulling Tracy into a dance with him, Cam doesn't bother to hide their laughter. This is what they have to look forward to for the rest of their lives, and they can't wait.

Holly Voss

Holly is a queer and nonbinary author that specializes in transformative fiction. They have been writing for over 20 years and show no signs of stopping. When not writing, Holly does their best to teach math to high schoolers. They generally end up learning just as much from their students as they manage to teach.

Mended

by Amanda Hill

It only took a moment to read the text from Eve. A moment too long. When I looked up, my tires straddled double yellow lines and a horn interrupted Folsom Prison Blues.

I swerved, missing the oncoming car by inches, but my reaction threw the car off-balance. Time slowed. I froze as the car tipped. Johnny sang about the railroad train, and then metal crunched like ice in a blender. A slam to my shoulder. A blow to my head. And then nothing.

When I became aware of my surroundings again, there were lights–blue and red behind my eyelids. Why couldn't I open them?

Small sharp rocks pricked the back of my skull, digging into my scalp. Darkness followed the blue light, then flashed again–dark, light, dark, light.

Pain in my left arm and head spiked with each breath. I couldn't feel my fingers.

Was this the end? Maybe I'd die. It would be better than surviving at this point. My kids would take my keys away again. Steal my freedom. They'd be disappointed just like they'd been the first time they stole the keys from me. Their shocked faces after I got a new set from the dealership made all the trouble worth it.

True, my driving skills had declined in the past few years, but I still had a license. I suspected that would change after today.

Movement and noise pierced the dark. Someone grabbed my wrist while another person slipped a pillow under my neck. All actions quick and precise against my still frame. Someone called out to me, waiting for a response, but I couldn't understand what they said, and my lips were as difficult to open as my eyes.

Amidst the noise, a familiar but troubling sound reached my ears, shooting adrenaline through the pain—a pair of scissors snipping the sweater I'd pulled on just hours before.

I'd never worn it until she died. Everything my wife made she did with precision, but sweaters weren't my thing. While I felt gratitude for her efforts on my behalf, I couldn't bring myself to put it on outside the house. I thought it made me look like an old man.

My lack of enthusiasm for the sweater ensured she stopped making them for me, and now this was the only one I'd ever have.

The cutting continued, and while I struggled to bring myself from the brink of awareness, tears pushed from my closed eyes with every snip.

In the months following her death, the sweater lay forgotten until the cold weather settled in. One fall morning, I noticed it at the bottom of a drawer and grabbed it. As I pulled the fabric over my head, I could see in my mind all the nights she'd spent knitting it. The yarn running through her hands, the needles clicking in rhythm. It never hit me before how much her hands had touched it—hands I only wished could touch me now.

Instead, unknown hands pulled my left sleeve off

while others slipped beneath my head and upper back. Someone lifted the sweater away, and I finally found the strength to cry out.

"Don't worry, we've got you," said the soft voice of a woman, her blurry figure beside me.

I didn't care who had me–who had the sweater?

I heard the rollers on the stretcher slide into place, then voices communicating vitals before I gave up and dropped into the darkness.

I woke to unfamiliar sounds. A nurse enclosed my arm in a pressure cuff and turned it on. Blood staunched inside my arm. My head pounded. I looked around, confused at the white walls and medical equipment hooked to my body.

"It's good to see you awake." The nurse smiled. "The doctor will be in soon to update you on your condition."

My condition?

All at once, memories of the accident flooded back in–the sounds of the horn and squealing tires. The crunching metal and the cold scissors against my skin, cutting.

My wife had touched every square centimeter of that sweater. She'd thought of me with every stitch, poured her intentions into the piece, and it became an extension of her love. It held off the chill in the air and softened the cold in my heart, and now it was gone.

After she took my vitals and left, Eve's voice surprised me from the corner. "Dad," she said as she came to my bed and took my hand. "We were so worried. Can't you see why you can't drive anymore? We could have lost you."

"Of course, we couldn't wait too long to point out

you were right." She blushed, and I smiled to soften my words. I hated it, but I knew they were looking out for me. "Do you know where they put my sweater?"

She rubbed her hand along my bald head. "Don't worry about that, Dad. Let's get you recovered. We can worry about the sweater later."

I tried to argue but found I'd already drained what little energy I had upon waking.

Eve made sure I was comfortable and tried to offer me food, but I closed my eyes and didn't answer.

A doctor woke me sometime later, spouting information on bruises and fractured bones, warning me about my driving, insisting I'd been lucky. It should have been worse. My mind ran in too many directions to focus on what he said, and I interrupted his recovery instructions.

"What about the other car?" Before the accident, I couldn't imagine anything worse than losing the freedom to drive. Now I was facing the possibility I'd taken someone else's life.

The doctor placed his hand on my shoulder. "They were fine. The car ran off the road, and the driver got a good scare, but there were no injuries."

Relief filled my chest, leaving only the familiar grief that had been my companion for months. But now, I didn't have her sweater to ease it.

Brandon sat with me that evening, having less to say than Eve. My son inherited my reticence to prattle on, and we sat in silence. I felt terrible for taking time away from his family and job.

"Did you see where my sweater went?" I asked.

"I think Eve has it," he said.

We watched television together until I fell asleep.

The next day, Eve and Brandon argued in hushed

voices by the door. Brandon lost it first, forgetting to keep his voice down.

"Who said you could make that decision?"

"You think I have to ask your permission?" Eve stood taller. "You heard him asking about it yesterday."

"Will you two ever stop fighting?" When they were kids, I wondered if they'd kill each other before adulthood.

My voice still sounded as gravelly as the pavement that had left marks on my scalp.

"Sorry to wake you." Brandon shot Eve a pointed look. "We'll let you rest now."

Eve, ignoring him, moved to the side of my hospital bed and took my hand. "There's someone we'd like you to meet, Dad."

Brandon's lips tightened into a thin line. "Not now."

"Hearing you two fight is worse than being woken up." I looked at Eve and gestured to my standard-issue hospital gown. "I'm not in the best condition to meet anyone."

"See?" Brandon threw up his hands.

"You'll want to hear what she has to say," Eve said, looking straight into my eyes. She knew I could never say no to her.

Brandon's face turned a deeper shade of red. "I don't think he does."

I looked up at my son, who was too much like myself. "We might as well get it over with."

Brandon swore.

"Who is this person you want me to meet?"

Eve's smile lit up her face, making me glad I'd caved to her wishes. "Her name is Amelia. She's waiting in the lobby. I'll text her." She pulled her phone out of her pocket. "That's all I'm going to say. She can tell you more."

"It's just a passenger from the other vehicle," Brandon said, clearly proud of himself for ruining Eve's surprise.

A passenger from the other vehicle? My heart sped up and the room felt hot. Had they come to yell at me? I couldn't blame them. Would they accept my apologies? My eyes blinked over and over as I imagined all the possibilities. Would they press charges?

"We'll give you some privacy while you visit." Eve kissed me on the cheek and pulled Brandon out the door.

I should have listened to Brandon.

I licked my dry lips, wondering if I could pretend to be asleep, when a short woman with gray hair shuffled into the room, carrying a cotton bag nearly half her size. Her shoes were sensible, but her clothing tailored to fit. Large earrings hung past her chin, stretching her lobes so far only a thread of skin held the hooks in place.

"I'm Amelia," she said before she'd gotten two steps into the room. "I was a passenger in the other car. I'm so glad to meet you."

I took in a breath. "I'm sorry."

She held up her hand to stop me. "No need for apologies. That's not why I'm here."

She sat in the chair next to my bed, putting her bag on the floor. Though her voice warbled, it held a comforting cadence that somehow eased the tightness in my chest.

"In all my years, I've never witnessed such a terrible accident." Her voice cracked. "I thought you'd died." Her eyes glistened as she pulled a bottle of water from her bag to take a sip.

I looked away, unsure what to do about a stranger

becoming emotional over my well-being.

"I felt such relief when one of the paramedics said you were breathing. I'd been praying you'd pull through. When they pulled out the scissors to cut your sweater, I noticed it was hand-knit."

She pulled out a ball of yarn attached to a set of knitting needles from her bag. "I'm a knitter myself." She began moving the needles in practiced motions, all her focus on me, not the stitches.

"My heart broke again when they started cutting your sweater, and I wasn't surprised when you cried out." She leaned closer, "I understood what you wanted, but no one else seemed to notice."

How was it a stranger could understand me so well? While I was grateful for her sympathy, I didn't appreciate her showing up to open the wound again.

She set the needles down, reached into her bag again, and pulled from its depths a folded, navy blue garment.

I recognized it instantly, and my vision blurred.

"I tried seaming it back together, but the yarn was so thick it kept unraveling along the edge. It didn't look good." She stated it with authority born from years of experience.

She unfolded the sweater and held it up for me to see, though my tears and lack of glasses made it hard to discern much detail.

"Instead, I took the liberty of finishing the ends and turning it into a cardigan." She set it next to me on the bed. "I hope it's okay. I know it's not the same, but it won't unravel when you wear it."

I pulled the sweater in, holding it to my nose. The familiar smell of wool dominated, but a floral scent wove itself through the fibers. The same sweater, but new.

"I'm sorry if I caused family discord." She glanced at the door. "I approached your daughter about fixing the sweater, and she gave it to me right away." She sat back in her chair, picking up her knitting again, fingers and needles flying together in a dance. "When your son found out, he . . ." she pursed her lips, "wasn't happy about it."

I chuckled, surprised at how quickly she'd changed my mood. I tried to say thank you, to tell her not to worry about Brandon, but my words came out distorted with emotion.

She understood me anyway.

"No need to thank me, it was my pleasure." She stopped knitting, put her work back in the bag, and stood up.

Before she'd entered the room, the only thing I needed for my world to make sense was the sweater she'd just given me. But I felt myself unravel as she walked toward the door.

I opened my mouth, a plea for her to stay formulating on my tongue, but a sudden fear choked out the words. Why would she want to stay with me? We'd only just met. How could I ask more of her after what she'd already done?

Her hand rested on the doorknob. In moments she'd be gone for good. It would be easy to do nothing, but if I didn't say something, would she ever understand what she'd done for me?

A fearful voice inside whispered now was not the time. I needed rest; Amelia had better places to be—we were strangers.

But I knew there would never be another time. If I didn't act now, I wouldn't get a second chance.

"Wait." The word came out scratchy, but it stopped her. She turned to look at me, and again I didn't know what to say. I wished I could have come up with something genius, but all I managed to say was, "You like to knit?"

Next, I could ask her if she liked big earrings.

Instead of laughing, she shuffled back to her chair, pulled out her knitting, and said, "Almost as much as you like to surf the pavement."

I smiled, and we began a conversation that lasted for years.

Amanda Hill

Amanda Hill's passion for writing is second only to her passion for reading. Accolades include winning First Place in the New Voices Fiction category with the League of Utah Writers, and being published in their anthology. When she isn't writing or reading, she is knitting her way through closets of yarn, or supporting arts in the community by costuming plays, or volunteering for art programs in local schools. She lives in South Jordan, Utah with her husband and five children.

The Last Chance

by Johnny Worthen

Ruth watched the car pull into the parking lot and knew even before it had stopped, turned off its lights, and disgorged its single inhabitant into the flickering glow of the failing neon sign, that fate had crossed them again.

It was some kind of galactic weave, some strange unification of fates that kept touching her life to his. She'd noticed it before, commented on it, pondered it, even wrote about it in her diary, always with regret and a sense of failed destiny. It was coincidence, of course, the product of a small suburb and his rise to fame—a thing of perspective and confirmation bias, but still a nagging annoyance she could not help but fixate upon.

So it was that she was not at all surprised to see Pierce Malman step out of a rented car, and after straightening the lines of his tailored gray suit and running his fingers through his tousled black hair, march to the door of the cafe and come in.

The Last Chance Cafe was a landmark and a dive. For half a century it had never closed, catering to early risers, lunch crowds, and the midnight denizens who needed food at 3:00 a.m. It smelled of coffee and bacon, syrup, eggs, and clandestine cigarettes. Hard-earned sweat. It had been made over several times, the most recent dating it by a decade with now-worn carpet and stained ceiling tiles. The lights always seemed brighter at night when the darkness outside was so thick. It stood as a beacon and harbor off Sixteenth Street, a pensive rest stop to refuel, recoup, and re-assess. It was a pocket of slow time, especially so late as this, a place to catch up before moving on.

It was 3:05 a.m.

Ruth had worked at the cafe for four years and would see it to the end. The new Denny's by the freeway had finally nailed the Last Chance Cafe's coffin shut, and unless it found a buyer within the month, it would be closed in two.

Pierce Malman—Senator Pierce Malman—blinked at the bright lights in the foyer and took in Ruth standing behind the counter next to the register. He saw and didn't see her. The waitress uniform was unremarkable, the lined face with little make-up was hard and nondescript. Thin and sinewy, so clothed and bedecked, she stood the very form of a functionary.

"A booth," he said.

Ruth took a single menu out of the box, wiped it with moist towel smelling of maple syrup, and without asking if he was alone or meeting someone, a common question in the day but insulting at night, she showed him to the back of the cafe to a corner booth where he spread out like an ooze and ordered coffee with four eggs over hard with toast without touching the menu.

"And a water," he said, finally making eye contact with Ruth.

His eyes were bloodshot-normal, the standard for customers at this time of night, and they showed no sign of recognition.

"Coming up," she said and went back to the kitchen.

Pierce took out his phone and scrolled through his messages. His mind fell back to Debby, his mistress, for just a brief moment, and he remembered leaving her on the bed in the apartment that he paid for, sleeping in a knot of red satin sheets he required her to use. It was the briefest memory of drink, drugs, and sex. Rutting. Slaps. Sleep, then awake in the dark, needing to be gone.

Already congratulations had begun to flood in. His name had only been floated, not even announced, and already people were coming out of the woodwork to ride his coattails.

He looked up to see the waitress placing a glass of water on the table.

"You want me to leave the pitcher?" she asked.

"Where's the coffee?" he said.

"We're brewing a new pot. You wouldn't want to touch what we had, Senator."

"You recognize me." He smiled. "That speaks highly of my constituency."

"I know you," she said. "Do you remember me?"

He looked at her now, blinking against the fluorescent backlight.

"Give me a hint."

"I'm Ruth Merriweather. I sat behind you in school."

"That's taking me back." He slipped into his patented capped smile, the one he used at work to get votes.

"You invited me to Senior Prom," she said.

"I don't think so. I went with Becky Sommors."

"You did. You asked me first and then canceled to go with Becky."

His smile slipped. "I don't recall."

"I went with Steve Caldeman," she said. "It worked out. I married him."

"I love stories like that."

"I was kind of mad at the time."

"Well . . ."

"I didn't like Becky so much either," she said, "so after all that, it was, you know, confusing."

"Coffee's up!" came a call from the kitchen and Ruth left to fetch it.

He recalled the prom, "all that" so many years ago. Before the new movements. Before the new politically correct inquisition of modern times. What he had done was hardly out of the ordinary in those days and it came down to a he-said-she-said situation that hadn't survived graduation. Becky had a reputation going in, and he was popular. It wasn't like he'd taken anything that she hadn't already given away.

"Do I know that guy?" asked Carlos in the kitchen.

"That's Senator Malman," said Ruth.

"He's been in the news, right?"

"Short-listed for a Supreme Court seat."

"Shit."

"Yes," she said and took the coffee.

Becky had been the first time. Ruth hadn't seen it then, didn't understand what was happening. Had she done research then she might have recognized the rising pattern, but she had her own life and that was theirs—their problems, their accusations and denials. As such, it became the first point on the map of coincidence that led to today.

Pierce considered leaving the cafe, getting the hell out of this shit-house town of an old suburb, and getting back to Washington by an earlier flight. He'd left this town behind him after high school and only remained a citizen of it because its voting bloc was so secure. Once he got his seat—his lifetime appointment—he could finally flush this place, for good and all.

Ruth placed cream, sugar, and sweeteners next to the heavy white porcelain cup before filling it with fresh coffee.

"You've done quite well," she said. "The best of our class by far."

"I'm just here to serve."

"It was the Senchezi case that really skyrocketed you, wasn't it?"

"Everyone deserves a defense," he said, somewhat defensively.

"I was actually a reporter at that time," she said. "I was in the courtroom for much of it."

Again, he tried to see her as someone he knew. Thirty years ago, now twenty. "Did you wear your hair differently then?" he asked.

"I sure did," she giggled. "I was kind of a radical."

"Who were you a reporter for?"

"The People's Standard."

He laughed. "Wow."

"Yeah, I know, right?" She laughed too. "Could hardly put that on my resume after the arrests."

"No." He drank his coffee black.

"They did get a little sensational," she said. "Probably had it coming after doxing the police force, but the Senchezi case I thought was handled well."

"Because you were writing it?"

She smiled warmly, her patented uncapped smile. The one she used at work to get tips. "Exactly."

There was a pause while they both remembered the

case, and then she turned and went looking for his eggs.

Senchezi had killed three anti-police protestors and wounded eight, with his modified assault rifle on a cloudy April afternoon. The shooting had been live-streamed by no fewer than eight witnesses, most from the "law and order" side. After a long time, the police finally approached and arrested him. The perp walk of him being taken to a police car, still with his rifle over his shoulder and eating a bag of Doritos given him by the deputy, made international news.

Defense attorney Pierce Malman had led his defense and got him acquitted. There were details and techni-calities, charges of withholding evidence and tampering with some, plus a thick dose of blaming the victims. Senchezi walked. It had been a revelation to Pierce then. Before the verdict he'd wondered about the world, and his place in it. But after it, all of those existential ques-tions were gone. The world was as the clever made it. Morality and justice were smokescreens to be negotiated and ignored when opportunities arose. It was a dog-eat-dog world and he was a big dog.

There were riots following the acquittal, and talk of a retrial, more police brutality, more international outrage, but early snows put down the protests and Senchezi died before Christmas. He blew himself up in his parents' basement while making a bomb. The blast killed six peo-ple: his parents, three neighbors, and himself.

For his part in the trial, Malman became famous in some circles, infamous in others. A self-proclaimed light-ning rod. Unrepentant, unbowed. A guy who got things done. His fame carried him through to a House Seat, thanks to this secure district.

Ruth put the eggs on the table and refilled the coffee

mug.

"We crossed a third time," she said out of the blue, "when you broke ground for the Barger Development in what used to be the Three Creeks Wilderness District."

"That's a hell of a way to say it," he said. "Sounds like you're still working for The People's Standard."

"Oh, I've grown out of that," she said. "Reality is reality. Ideals like those are for the young and foolish, those who can afford to think past their next paycheck."

"Reality does tend to make people conservative."

"I remembered at the time watching you with that silver shovel, me and Steven and little Ted, our son."

"Wondering what?"

"Wondering how I kept running into you at these big moments."

"Prom?"

"And the trial, and the end of the wilderness, and the war."

"The war hadn't happened then."

"No," she said absently. "No, not yet. Teddy was so young then. But I remember looking at the wilderness, knowing that it was a land grab for a mine, and not the affordable housing it was sold as."

"Land is to use, girl," he said. "Barger found a better use for it."

"You know it's a Superfund site now, right?"

"Is it?"

"Yeah."

"Hmm."

"Enjoy your breakfast." She left him alone.

He'd made out pretty well with the Barger deal. A couple million in fact. It was how he became a Senator. The Wilderness had been nice, but the oil and lead pulled out of it had been far more economically impact-ful than the tourists looking for that endangered—no, now extinct—woodpecker. A lot of people got rich on that deal—none from that district of course, except him-self.

"It's about being in the right place at the right time," he said out loud to the empty table. Hearing his own voice, he looked around to see that he was alone. He laughed at his outburst, fatigue getting to him. "Timing," he said to wrap it up. "Success is about being bold, see-ing the opportunities and taking them."

"Is it?"

He jumped. Ruth was there with a dessert menu.

"I didn't see you come up."

"The cafe has a way of concealing things," she said. "These late hours are strange."

"Yeah."

"My son died in the war," she said.

"Which one?"

"Yours?"

"What?"

"Sorry," she said. "I've been on my feet all day. Let me get you a free piece of pie. What kind would you like?"

"Lemon."

She left, taking the menu with her.

It hadn't been his war. He only helped bring it about. How long could his country suffer the indignities of hav-ing their noble soldiers attacked for no other crime than that of having a base in their country?

It had been a quick war. He'd made eight figures in contributions and speaking fees, some he didn't even have to attend. The country had another puppet dictator in a strategic area. It had only cost a few hundred American lives. A few tens of thousands of theirs. Okay, maybe it was fair to call it his war. He'd been the flag-bearer for much of the debate. It made him a superstar with the party and got his name bantered around for the Big Job. Dogs eat dogs.

From across the cafe, Ruth watched Malman. He was the only customer. She and Carlos, the only employees. The morning staff would come in at 5:00. She calculated the minutes and again measured the times she had crossed paths with Pierce Malman.

While selling the war, he'd spoken at a rally in Arizona. It was surreal. She was there on her way back from Mexico where she'd bought medicine that would slow Steve's death but not stop it. Ted was already in Basic, the only way forward to get to college and that architecture degree he'd wanted. Steve's cancer was incurable—had been from the first moment it'd been diagnosed since they couldn't afford the cure. Their insurance company denied the claim, and fighting it became as expensive as the treatment, leaving them bankrupt within a year. She recalled noticing in the middle of all that, watching Malman on CSPAN as he filibustered the Insurance Commitment Act that would have saved her husband. But there in Arizona, on the tarmac, as Malman spoke, while she worried about customs finding the pills in her suitcase, she saw the coming war and found a new fear with her son's face on it.

Malman was an eloquent speaker. He could move audiences. And juries, she remembered. He could make the ridiculous sound plausible and rouse hidden depths of hatred and fear to the cause.

The people Senchezi had killed were black, Puerto Rican, and gay. The ones he wounded, liberals. He was white. How could he not have taken action in the face of such effrontery?

The war enemy was again brown, possessing worthless land between an oligarch's oil field and another oligarch's port. The papers didn't say that of course. It was about patriotism and pride. The attack that instigated the cry was suspicious in a Gulf of Tonkin kind of way, but what of it? America, right or wrong, and Malman sold it. He could have been a preacher. He had a talent. Listening to him in the customs line, miraculously unsearched, she could only stare in awe at her old classmate.

The coincidences piled up in her mind then. There in Arizona the pattern became clear, and for the first time it led her to an action. Not that she took it, but she saw it, saw the suggestion of what to do and colored it with the shades of missed opportunities and resulting events.

She couldn't of course. Steve needed her. She was a mother. She worked three jobs. She had responsibilities. She had too much to lose. And he was far away.

"Our children's children will thank us for what we do," he'd said that day at the Airport. "It should not— cannot be put off. If we do not act now, it will only be worse later."

Cheers from the crowd. She marveled at all the cleanly printed signs the crowd held up for him at this, his "unannounced" layover in Phoenix.

Steve had died that year. Ted the year after. Three years after that, she had but one job and a hip that would need surgery within the year if she intended on using it in the next.

It was easy for her there in the bright cafe in the dark night to assemble the pieces of the puzzle, to connect the moments and the consequences, the certain realization of barriers and opportunities. Synchronicity.

She limped a little as she carried the lemon pie to the table before collecting the dirty dishes.

Pierce cringed at her presence, waiting for more of her attitude, but she only smiled that smile and he gave her his before sipping more coffee.

When she was gone, he leaned back and contemplated the pie wondering why he was here. It wasn't like him to lurk these late hours. Insomnia was not his way. He concluded the cocaine must have been laced with uppers and he was excited about the coming nomination.

This would be better than the Big Job, which would be scrutinized and short-lived. He was getting tired of the scrutiny, the pageant, the pretend concern for people he despised. The Supreme Court—now there was a place to make a difference long term. There were hot cases coming up that made him salivate; abortion—the perennial, but also voting rights and property rights that would set precedent for decades if not centuries. He'd be able to weigh in on the Barger case, which was now at the Appellate Court. Best of all, he'd be the swing vote for the qualified immunity question. That is to say, he could remake the country in his own image. A smooth-running machine headed by the right people. The big dogs.

He was smart enough to understand this. Though his handlers from the party, from the administration, even the big guy himself, talked in circles and analogies, he knew what was going on. There was a quick window now before the next congress was seated where he could be put into place and secure the high court with little trouble.

The announcement was forthcoming; his midnight

texts told him news was already out.

He decided to go back early to DC, be seen with the wife when the reporters came looking for him. He'd sleep on the plane.

"Bring me the bill," he called to the waitress who nodded from the back of the cafe near the bus table, where she and some Mexican were talking, probably about him by the way they cast glances his way. Such it was to be famous.

He watched the waitress follow the man into the back and after a moment return, and approach his table with the check.

"Is your friend there legal?" he asked her.

"I've never asked," she said, tearing off the ticket and placing it face down on the table.

"You should ask. It's your duty as a citizen," he said.

"My duty as a citizen?" She smiled broadly. "What?"

Ruth produced Carlos' gun from her right front pocket, leveled it at Pierce Malman's forehead, and fired the single bullet that killed him at 3:46 a.m.

Johnny Worthen

Johnny Worthen is an award-winning, multiple-genre, tie-dye-wearing author, voyager, and damn fine human being! Trained in literary criticism and cultural studies, he writes upmarket fiction, long and short, mentors others where he can and teaches at the University of Utah. He is a past President of the League of Utah Writers and Utah Writer of the Year.

Pioneering Final Frontiers

by C. H. Lindsay

ΔΔΔ
Transfixed,
the young girl
stares at the screen
as one man's small step
changes her tomorrows.

From Apollo
to Atlantis.
Skylab, SpaceX,
ISS, Mir.

When grown,
the girl will
circle the earth,
the moon, and beyond—
the stars her destiny.

Now, in her dreams
of Saturn 5,
she's Lost in Space
on Enterprise.

One day,
from Moonbase
Alpha, her girl
will help colonize
Jupiter's moons and Mars.

Pioneering
final frontiers
is still the hope
of those who dream.
ΔΔΔΔΔ

C. H. Lindsay

Charlie is an award-winning poet & writer, housewife, and book-lover. She currently has short stories and poems in eleven anthologies, with two more coming out next year. Her works have appeared in several magazines, including Amazing Stories and Space and Time Magazine. She is working on three novels, five short stories, and two dozen poems (so far).

In 2018 she became her father's literary executor. She now publishes his four books under Carlisle Legacy Books, LLC, with plans to add more books in the coming years.

She is a member of SFWA, HWA, SFPA, and LUW. She is a founding member of the Utah Chapter of the Horror Writers Association.

Bioengineering the End of the World

by Bradley S. Blanchard

Day 1 of 4

The scream slammed into Parthus. Dropping the box of notebooks and papers, he raced up the basement stairs. Arianna lay on the kitchen floor, in an oversize t-shirt and black sweatpants. She was holding her large, round belly, her breathing rapid and shallow.

"The baby." She looked up at him with big brown eyes framed by a face of indeterminate years. Parthus felt the blood drain from his face. The baby was premature—early, too early.

"Fall detected. Do you require help?" A chipper digital assistant asked.

"Yes," she said. "Emergency. Labor contractions."

"Car en route. Arrival in eighty-seven seconds. Connecting to nearest hospital."

A shiny, red self-driving car waited for them in the driveway. The car opened its doors, buckled them in, and took over the hospital call. While the nurse scanned Arianna's vitals from the vidscreen, the car sped past the neighborhood park.

The park grass was a perfect height, trimmed by touchless, solar-powered mowers. Couples walked through the flower gardens. All half dozen chessboards were in use, set to the music of people playing on the nearby basketball court and a party over by the pond.

The park had no graffiti. No broken bottles. No trash. No swings, slides, or merry-go-rounds. No old men sitting on benches to feed the pigeons. No grandmothers pushing grandchildren in strollers. No teenagers killing time. No old. No young. No babies. No children.

Parthus slumped onto a vinyl couch in the hospital waiting room. He didn't want to watch the C-section. It was early, only thirty-two weeks along. Not that it mattered. Early. Late. Its survival was a statistical improbability.

He flipped through his notebook, looking at formulas. He'd started his research after the second baby had died. Sixteen years' worth of experiments and all he had to show for it was a third dead child and a fourth now tipping over into the grave.

A nurse in scrubs, with the young, unguessable age synonymous with the Matilda Virus, walked up. The digital assistant identified her as Arianna's nurse.

"You can go see your wife now," she said. "Most people try once. Some try twice, but you're on try four. That's got to be some kind of record." Parthus gave her a tight-lipped smile and exited the waiting room.

Mercy General was like most hospitals. It had an emergency room, a set of surgical suites, and a maternity ward. However, unlike most hospitals, it also had a Newborn Intensive Care Unit, NICU for short.

When he reached Arianna's room, she was lying in the bed, dozing.

"Have you seen the baby yet?" he asked, sitting down

next to her and taking her hand. Arianna nodded and smiled. "She's beautiful. I named her Gabriella."

"Why did you name it?" They had talked about this, about not getting attached. It was like pouring all your love into a mayfly, hoping it would live longer than one day. The brief lives of these babies were matches in a twilight world of shadows that only made everything seem all the darker when they sputtered out and died.

"Everything deserves a name. She's going to make it. I can feel it. She'll fill our house with laughter and grow up to be amazing. Go see her."

Parthus shook his head no, but as it always did with Arianna, his will slipped, and soon he was on his way to see the child.

At the NICU there were more than a dozen babies in little bassinets. Some had numbers, most had names, all had a whiteboard with big red numbers ranging between one and four.

A nurse offered a smile more placating than hopeful. She wore scrubs, but no mask. There was no point in masks.

The baby was over in the corner. The board read "Gabriella: 1." Parthus stood over it. Dozens of little white dots, no bigger than a pinhead, covered it, monitoring everything that happened. The scanners read the health of the Matilda Virus. Newborns showed up as green; healthy people were a bright purple; dead people were black; there were no other colors and no other variations.

The thing was about the size of a cabbage. It would be dead before the weekend and leave an emotional wreck behind that would take a decade to clean up. He studied its face, felt the stirrings of affection, and left the room. You couldn't let yourself get attached. You just couldn't.

The Matilda Virus created a practically immortal population that was already straining the earth's resources. You couldn't keep adding people. Infant deaths were an accepted side effect of the Matilda Virus. Less than one baby in a million beat the odds, and all the monitoring from the last forty years hadn't changed that statistic one decimal.

Day 2 of 4

Parthus stopped off at the hospital on his way to work. Arianna was sleeping. He went to see the baby, but only because he knew Arianna's digital assistant would inform her he had been at the hospital.

"Two-minute countdown," he told his phone. Anything shorter would be hard to defend to Arianna. He stood over the baby, waiting on the timer. After half a minute, he pulled over a rocking chair. At sixty seconds it stirred. Parthus ignored it. At two minutes he stood up. It stirred and looked at him with dark, round eyes. They looked like Arianna's.

The hook sunk deep into his heart and he cursed his wife, getting a dirty glance from a nurse. He knew this would happen. He couldn't get attached.

The baby closed her eyes, and he sat down. It was like watching the tide recede down the beach, hoping it would come back. He studied the little face.

"What's that tune?" the nurse asked. Parthus hadn't realized he had been humming.

"A lullaby my mother sang to me when I was little." He didn't bother to add it was about raising your voice when the still night ended to greet a new day. He stood up to go, embarrassed he'd let himself get ensnared, and hurried to the door.

As he was pushing it open, an alarm split the air. He turned around and was three steps back into the room when he realized it wasn't Gabriella that was in trouble. At the far end of the room, a baby was convulsing. The whiteboard read "Leesa: 4." Her monitor was dimming from green to black. Nurses flooded the room. All the babies, including Gabriella, had opened their eyes wide at the alarm, but none of them made a sound. Another side effect of the virus. Not a cry. Not a gurgle. Not a peep. Not even Leesa, whose body thrashed about in silence.

"You've seen the lab results. The entire group died."

Jenn, Arianna's younger sister, was a sixty-four-year-old in the body of a thirtysomething. Jenn had looked for a cure after the first baby died. Parthus hadn't gotten serious until after the second, when he realized Arianna would not stop until one survived or the weight of the collective tragedies broke her.

"Bright side," said Parthus. "Survival rate moved from four days to five."

"In monkeys. Still not ready for human testing. Human testing makes it immediately political."

"We have three days," Parthus said. "Politicians don't act that fast."

"Security services do." She said. "Soldiers destroyed all of Dr. Ostopapa's research within twenty-four hours. Scientific luminary one day, professional black hole the next."

He nodded, ceding the point.

"Parthus, everyone says the Matilda Virus is present

in newborns but doesn't attach, and that's what kills the baby. But, what if it does attach and just can't keep up with their growth?"

"That's not what the studies show."

"Government studies. Dr. Ostopapa's was privately funded."

He shot her a glance, and she fell silent. It was a wonderful world, but everything listened. Phones. Jewelry. Clothes. Parthus pushed the button on top of a small box. A light flashed. The box disrupted all electronics in the area, forcing them to reconnect. They had about sixty seconds.

"I thought they destroyed all her research," he said.

"I found a paper, an incomplete draft. She speculates physical growth rate is the key."

"You know, Dr. Matilda Wilson once hinted at something similar." Parthus walked to the whiteboard. He grabbed a green marker and started filling the board with formulas. "I actually wrote her once, on a piece of paper. She wrote me back the same way. Blue ink, just like her color on the scanner. I got the letter just a few days before she died."

"I thought there were only three colors."

"Only three now, but she made it sound like there were four at some point."

"How old is the formula you're putting up?" Jenn asked.

"Over ten years. Inspired by Dr. Wilson. After baby three died—"

"You mean Marcus."

"That's what I said. After baby three, it just kind of stalled." That time was fuzzy in his normally flawless memory, one long shadowy blur of loss.

"When Marcus died," Jenn said, "I thought we were going to lose Arianna too. She crashed so hard." The red light in the box was flashing faster. "I hate this. Why can't we just study the Virus directly instead of tiptoeing around it? We'll never get anywhere this way. Not soon enough to do anything useful."

Parthus stopped writing. "Maybe that's the point."

The Matilda Virus was off-limits to direct study. Officially, they were studying indirect effects, like how to stop it from changing genetically manipulated hair colors in grown adults.

"You know Dr. Wilson died of old age," Parthus said, "along with her brother and daughter."

"Why?"

"Immune to her own virus."

"That would be something worth studying."

The light in the box had stopped blinking. He tapped it again, forcing another reset. It was suspicious to have everything reset twice. Parthus hoped it would be overlooked.

"What if Dr. Ostopapa was right," Jenn said. "What if newborn babies are developing so rapidly the virus can't keep up?"

He considered it aloud. "Fast enough to halt development, but too slow to rebuild. Like a gardener who prunes the original tree branches but doesn't have time to graft in new branches, and just keeps pruning until, eventually, the tree dies."

"We just need to slow the virus down long enough for natural growth to occur."

"A reversion?" He turned back to the incomplete formulas on the whiteboard, erased them, dredged new ones from his memory, and started writing again.

"A temporary reversion."

"How?"

"You're the theoretical genius. You tell me."

"I wish I knew where her letter was," Parthus said.

"You know we're far beyond the scope of our grant."

The light on the small box was flashing a warning. They only had a few seconds before everything started listening again.

"Regrets?"

"Not if it works, but we're on day two. There's not enough time to get approval, let alone run another test."

The light on the small box went solid red. Everything reconnected. His earphone chirped to life. Arianna's panicked voice came through.

"Something is wrong with Gabriella. Get down here. You need to get down here!"

"I'll be right there," Parthus said.

"No, now! Not after you finish some stupid formula. We need you now."

When they reached Arianna's room, her eyes were puffy from crying.

"What happened?"

"I was holding Gabriella. The alarm sounded. She shook in my arms. She went from green to black. Then nurses were everywhere and took her from me." Arianna looked up at him, teetering on the edge of a bottomless abyss of despair.

"I'll find her," he said. "I'll do . . . something."

He stood up and Jenn took his place at Arianna's side. Parthus headed down the hall to the NICU. The babies were all silent. The whiteboard still said "Gabriella: 2." Her bassinet was still empty.

He grabbed a nurse. "Where did that baby go?" He pointed to the empty bassinet.

The nurse listened to her earphone, then responded, "I don't have any news right now. If you'll return to your wife's room, we'll let you know when there is news."

Unwilling to go back to Arianna with that answer, he wandered the hospital looking for a way into the surgical suites. Heading down a small corridor he hadn't noticed before, he ended up at a thick metal door that required a badge. The door opened, a blast of cold air hit him, and a man emerged. Behind the man, on a small metal gurney, was a little body covered with a sheet. Parthus stomach knotted up.

"What's its name?" Parthus asked, desperation filling his voice.

"Who?"

"The baby. That baby," he said, his voice thick with anger.

"Leesa." The man glanced up at a camera and hurried down the hall.

Joy and relief flooded through Parthus. It wasn't Gabriella.

He thought of the formulas, written in green pen, when baby number four was born. Arianna had named it Marcus. Parthus never saw it. It died on Day 2. Dr. Wilson's letter had arrived a few days before and he felt so close to a solution that he couldn't leave the lab, not yet. Then both Dr. Wilson and the baby had died, along with the inspiration driving that set of formulas.

Clarity cut through the gloom. He had written the formulas in a spiral notebook and bookmarked them with the letter. They were in a box in the basement.

At the house, he found an "Inspection Warrant" posted on the front door, and civil security was carrying out boxes of his stuff.

"Excuse me," Parthus said to the supervisor. "What's going on?"

"Research review," she replied. "Sign the tablet on the table to get your items back when the review is complete."

He hurried past her to the basement, almost bowling over a man coming up with a box. Parthus scanned the box. A spiral-bound notebook peeked out from one corner. Parthus started to follow when something caught his eye. Tucked between two unopened boxes, for a stroller and a crib, was an envelope, addressed in blue ink. It must have fallen out when he'd dropped the box the day Arianna fell. Parthus hurried down the stairs and snapped up the letter. The return address was Dr. Matilda Wilson.

There was a creak at the top of the stairs. "Sir, I'll need you to sign this," the supervisor said. She looked at the letter.

"It's just a letter," Parthus said, hedging.

The officer held out her hand. Parthus hesitated.

"Please," he mouthed. Everything listened.

She read the name on the letter, then looked at the basement filled with piles of unopened baby items. "You sure you want to keep that piece of junk mail? I can throw it out for you," she said, with a catch in her voice.

"I may keep it for a while. Don't get mail like this anymore."

"No, you don't." Her soft voice became officious again. "Sign here."

Parthus looked up from the whiteboard as Jenn entered his office. It was almost midnight.

"Why did you leave?" Jenn demanded.

"Jenn, they took all my research."

"Gabriella is okay for the moment, thanks for asking. Arianna is not. How could you walk out on her like that? She needs you."

"It's a glorified hospice ward. No matter how much love and skill those nurses pour into that job, the babies all die."

"Some make it past day four."

"Not because of the doctors. They don't have the tools." He wrote, "They took all my research from the house," on the whiteboard.

The blood drained from her face. "Security or soldiers?" she mouthed.

He mimed writing on a tablet.

She grabbed a notebook and scribbled, "I need to call the team." A pause, then added, "Maybe we can still salvage this."

He tapped the box. The red light appeared.

"Jenn, in two days it won't matter anymore," he said, breaking the silence. He slid his notebook across to her. He had recreated the green formulas with blue corrections pulled from Dr. Matilda Wilson in the margins. "I was working on these when the baby, when," he stumbled over the name, "when Marcus died. All we're missing are the DNA sequences to plug in."

"I'm not sure about this, Parthus. What if we can't control the spread?"

"If not now, when? By this time tomorrow, Gabriella could be dead and our research destroyed."

Jenn was skimming the letter. "She used a nebulizer.

Shot was too concentrated. We have inhalers; maybe they'll work. Smaller dose. Fewer side effects. Her husband got feverish, better, finally collapsed under the strain, and died. It looks like a page is missing."

Parthus had pulled the page. The first version of the Matilda Virus had required a quarantine and a cover-up. Eleven people had died. He was afraid Jenn would back out if she knew the truth.

"We'll have to use what we've got. Can we do this without a team?" he asked.

Silence.

"Can we even get it made?" Parthus prodded.

"Automated system. I can put in a request and hope no one notices. The manufacturer won't ship it to a residence. It'll go to the lab."

"And then Security Services will have that too."

"One step at a time. I looked for data on Dr. Wilson's genome. They have erased anything useful on her family."

"Once the military gets involved, everything goes from review to deletion."

"True." Jenn stood up and started gathering her things. "You've done all you can do here. Get back to Arianna and Gabriella."

"But– "

"Now!"

Day 3 of 4

"I can't do this again." Arianna looked up at Parthus. "I needed you, and you went back to the lab. And for what? A notebook full of formulas that don't help anyone. You're supposed to fix this. After Teesha died, you said you would fix this."

"I'm—"

"But you didn't, and then Marcus died, and you weren't even here." She turned away, sobbing. "Who else has to die before you fix this?"

"No one," he said. "I'll fix this. I will fix this."

She looked at him. Her brown eyes were deep pools of tears or belief, either of which would drown him. He immediately regretted the promise.

"Take a seat, Parthus."

He took a seat across from Leticia, the grant administrator for their lab.

"Do you know why you're here?"

"Why can't we study the virus directly?"

"The Matilda Virus is the cornerstone of society. You know that. I read the lab reports. You're trying to change the Matilda Virus itself. The legal implications. The ethical implications. I don't even know where to begin. If it escaped . . ."

"It won't."

"You're brilliant enough you might pull that off. Then what? Will you pick which babies live and which ones die? We're at nine billion. How many more practically immortal people do you think the earth can sustain indefinitely?"

"People die every year from accidents."

"You're going to base how many babies get born on an accident table?"

"So we bioengineer them out of the Virus." Desperation had crept into his voice.

Leticia shook her head. "You've just created a perpetual underclass who grow up, get sick, and die, while their nine billion elders live their lives around them. Eventually, the world goes back to violence, war, and starvation. Pick any option you want, this doesn't end well."

"How long will the review take?"

Her voice held a tinge of regret. "Too long," she said.

That was code. His career had just gone the way of Dr. Ostopapa's.

His phone buzzed in his ear. Package incoming.

"Can I at least clean out my office?" he asked.

"I can give you to the end of the week."

Parthus hurried down to Jenn's lab. Maybe he could intercept the drone before it reached the lab. Two soldiers stood guard outside the door. His heart sank; they had upgraded the situation. One soldier was talking to the drone, the other held up his hand to Parthus. "No one gets in or out."

"What about my stuff in the locker room?"

"No one gets in or out."

Next to him, the drone protested. "I just need someone to sign for it."

"Nothing in or out," the other soldier told the drone.

Parthus turned to the drone. "I may know someone who can sign for your delivery."

Day 4 of 4

Parthus held the inhaler in his hand. It had taken Jenn the better part of twenty-four hours to get the right size. He'd visited Arianna and Gabriella, shredded Dr. Wilson's letter, deleted all the lab research. There would be no going back.

"You don't have to do this," Jenn said, glancing at the office door. They'd started with two vials. Their first attempt to smuggle one out had tripped an alarm. Jenn had to break it to avoid its capture, and today there were soldiers posted at her lab and his office.

After today they would take their place next to Dr. Ostopappa or Dr. Matilda Wilson. He picked up a green dry erase marker, considered it for a moment, and swapped it for a blue one.

"What happened to the monkeys, again?" he asked, glancing at the empty table. They had taken his box. There would be no more secrets.

"Ostopapa's? They all died."

"But how long did each phase last?" He resisted the urge to fill the whiteboard.

"One day of flu-like symptoms. Three days of heightened energy. That's the contagious phase. Then collapse. But we don't know if Dr. Wilson's research parallels that."

Parthus thought of Arianna, lying in her hospital bed, just staring at the wall when she wasn't crying, or staring at him with perfect, trusting eyes, and of Gabriella, lying in the NICU, dying in silence, like Leesa had.

"I'd feel better if we could control the transmission," he said, "instead of just . . ."

"We don't have to do this," Jenn replied. "You and Arianna could try again. We could keep working to reverse the virus piecemeal."

Jenn was trying to sound upbeat, but they both knew a basement lab and a handful of supercomputers wouldn't cut it. They needed actual resources. Parthus knew there wouldn't be another baby, just as he knew Gabriella's death would finally break Arianna. She would lose all will to live and die, emotionally first, and then physically.

"We're out of options, aren't we?"

Jenn nodded.

Parthus looked at the inhaler again. It might kill him.

Probably would kill him. But he would rather precede Arianna and Gabriella than follow them.

Parthus pocketed the blue marker and went into the small bathroom. He heard the office door open.

"We need to scan the room again," a soldier said. After yesterday, they were suspicious he and Jenn hadn't turned everything over.

"That's unnecessary." Jenn positioned herself between the soldier and the bathroom.

"Move, or I will move you."

Parthus stuck the inhaler into his mouth, pushed as much air as possible out of his lungs, then activated it, hoping it wouldn't kill him. The aerosol was cold, like taking a breath on a below-zero winter day, stinging all the way down.

The coughing fit started as his lungs tried to expel the virus, creating the mucus that was quickly clogging up his bronchial tubes. Parthus dropped the inhaler into the toilet as he heard booted feet approach. Flushing the toilet, he had another spasm and dry heaved into the toilet.

The soldier grabbed Parthus, pulled him up, and spun him around. They were close enough to feel one another's breath. The soldier stepped back and pulled out a health scanner.

"That's weird," the soldier commented to himself. "We'll use a different scanner." For the first time, Parthus realized it was hot in the little bathroom. He glanced in the mirror. Sweat gathered in a small wrinkle in his brow. They exited the small bathroom.

Jenn was waiting by the office door.

"Ma'am, open the door," the soldier ordered, wiping a hand across his sweaty forehead.

Jenn's eyes flicked to his forehead, and the soldier took

that moment to push past her. The soldiers scanned Parthus using another scanner.

"It's broken," the second soldier said. "Look at this," he motioned to his partner, "the reading is blue. Color must need to reset."

"Or he's actually sick," the first soldier said, eyeing Parthus.

"No one gets sick anymore, and why would the scanner show him as blue?" the second soldier shot back.

"We're headed to the hospital anyway," Jenn said. "We'll have him checked out there." Parthus noticed a small bead of sweat making its way down the second soldiers' cheek.

As he exited the building, he heard someone call his name. He turned to see Dr. Liu and slowed down. They exited the building together.

"Heard you flew too close to the sun and they pulled the plug," she said.

Parthus just nodded. His roiling stomach made him afraid to speak.

"I'm on my way to the airport now, speaking at a big international conference, but I'm glad I caught you." Before Parthus could stop her, Dr. Liu stepped forward and gave him a quick hug. "Tell Arianna hi for me. And, in a year or two, maybe. I always need good lab assistants."

"I'll tell her you said hi," Parthus said, as a car pulled up behind them. "Enjoy your trip." Dr. Liu smiled as a car pulled up next to her. She wiped the sweat from her brow and climbed in.

"Hospital," Jenn said as Parthus climbed in. "What if we made a mistake? What if it doesn't save Gabriella?"

A nurse appeared on the screen and scanned him.

"Not an intake," he said. "Going to visit my wife."

The nurse frowned. "Unusually high temperature. You're reading blue."

"Screen again onsite," Jenn pushed back. "The car is a little buggy."

"That's three blue scans reported," the nurse said. "Meet at the side entrance for quarantine."

"All transmissions off," Jenn said to the car. "How do you feel?"

"Not too bad," he said.

"Wrong answer. Stage one—twenty-four hours, remember? You got through it in," she glanced at her watch, "fifteen minutes. You could be dead in an hour. This is all wrong. We should be taking blood samples, running tests, and fixing you."

"We just need to infect Gabriella."

"Parthus, you could kill her."

"She'll be dead in a few hours anyway."

"You could kill the rest of us."

He said nothing.

When they reached the hospital, they overrode the car, forcing it to park instead of going to the side entrance. Parthus opened his door, but Jenn had laid back her seat. She struggled to keep her eyes open.

"Jenn, security is waiting at the far entrance."

"You can't go in. It's airborne; you'll infect the whole hospital. Look at you, you're aging rapidly."

The mirror showed he was no longer looked in the prime of life but looked closer to fifty. Soon he'd look much older than that.

"Why aren't you sweating?" He asked.

"I couldn't find anything on Dr. Wilson's genome, so I used my own. Must react differently. Parthus, we didn't just slow the virus. I think we broke it." She passed out.

Security hurried towards the car. He popped the phone out of his ear and dropped it on the seat. Ducking down, he moved through the parking lot around to an unwatched side door. Slipping in, he fought the urge to see Arianna and went straight to the NICU.

It was all so clear. Dr. Wilson had used her own genome, making her immune to her own virus, along with her closest relatives. Then, Jenn had used her own genome for the payload, hoping to make Arianna immune. Everyone else would age. The only question was how fast.

The NICU was empty of nurses when he entered. He kneeled next to Gabriella and sang her a lullaby. When he finished, he noticed the empty bassinet still read, Leesa: 4.

He moved over to another baby, named Jacob, and sang Jacob a lullaby, letting his breath wash over him. Then on to Elijah. Isabella. Evelyn. Mandala. Ekeesie. He made his way around the small nursery until a nurse stopped him.

"What do you think you're doing?" she asked, scanning him.

"Singing," Parthus said. "All babies like singing. Do you sing to them?"

"Well, no," the nurse admitted.

"If you won't, I will." He kneeled next to 2085962. Pulling out the blue dry erase marker, he wrote Melese. "Everyone deserves a name," he said.

"Security to NICU. Come with me, please," the nurse said.

Parthus ignored the nurse and sang Melese a lullaby. When he finished, he stood. The nurse tried to block him from going to the next baby. He stepped around her to the next bassinet. She pulled it away. She grabbed a second bassinet and pulled it away as well.

She was faster than he was, and soon she had a cluster of bassinets behind her. He stopped. His back hurt, his knees protested, his thoughts seemed clouded. He grew fixated on a bead of sweat growing on the nurse's brow.

An alarm sounded. Nurses flooded the room. Gabriella's scanner had turned blue. Then Elijah's. Then Isabela's. Across the room, they were all turning blue, even those the nurse had gathered away from him.

Security rushed in and grabbed him just as he fell. He felt weak. His heart was pounding in his chest. Sweat was pouring down his face. His vision grew dim but, before death took him, his ears caught the perfect sound of Gabriella breaking out into one long wailing cry. Followed by a second wail. From across the entire room, a chorus of crying babies filled his ears, breaking their silence and greeting the new day.

Bradley S. Blanchard

Brad has done several kinds of writing, both professionally and personally, across the years, but always comes back to speculative fiction for both reading and writing, because he finds nothing more interesting then a good "What if" story. When he's not writing he's doing other stuff, because you can only stare at a wall for so long before the wall stares back at you.

Tillicum

by Scott E. Tarbet

R eally? People used to eat these disgusting things two hundred years ago? Aimlee wrinkled her nose, flipped the bag over. Potato chips, sure. Plenty of those in her own century. But New York Deli Dill Pickle flavored? She shrugged and placed them in her shopping cart, itself another historical oddity in a month that had been full of relics. Dad might get a kick out of them.

A loudspeaker crackled overhead. "Hey folks, it's almost ten o'clock. Tillicum Outfitters Thriftway and Ace Hardware will be closing in five minutes. Please finish up your shopping and head on up to the registers." Five minutes—that was going to be cutting it close. Kneeling in front of the rack of chips to conceal her actions, Aimlee triggered the holo display in her palm and swiped to recall her drones.

All over the combination grocery, hardware store, and hunting outfitter, nano-sized robotic camera drones homed on the open canister in her jacket pocket. She hoped they had been active long enough to get a thorough ultra-def recording of every centimeter of this fascinating place.

"Help you find something, Miss?" The voice came from above and behind her. She cursed inwardly. Until now she had managed to avoid direct contact with the locals. How would they react to her? There were First Nations faces here, but she had seen none with multiracial ancestry like hers.

She clenched her fist, freezing the swarm. She stood, feigning nonchalance, and turned to face the aproned grocery clerk who had spoken. He was a kid, a year or two younger than her. High school, probably. Big grin. No face mask.

But it was early in the pandemic, she reminded herself. Most people, especially in rural areas like Tillicum, still resisted the habit. That would not come until the death toll neared the first of several disastrous peaks. Now, early in the first wave, it was months away. An unarmed black man had been murdered by police, and the resulting Black Lives Matter protests had everyone on edge. The riots, the martial law, the bitterly-contested election, the riot at the U.S. Capitol that began the Second Civil War—all that was still to come. But those disasters were the responsibility of other time teams from the Smithsonian and the History Channel. Aimlee's family got to focus on the immersive VR of the lost bucolic splendor of the Olympic Peninsula. The viewers were going to eat it up.

"Nah," she said, biting her lip under her own anti-viral nanobot mask, and carefully remembered the dialect coaching that had preceded the mission. "No big deal. Just looking for the bigger bag of these." She indicated the pickle chips.

"Afraid that's the biggest size we've got," said the boy. His face brightened and he reached for another bag, peeled a store coupon from a pad on the edge of the shelf, and held them out to her. "Two-fer," he grinned.

"Twice the chips for the price of a single bag."

"Oh. Thanks." She placed them in the cart.

"I'm Quin," said the boy, holding out his hand. Aimlee drew a deep breath and suppressed a shudder. Shaking hands with a stranger was a social ritual she had only learned about in preparation for the time jump.

"I'm Aimlee." With an effort, she forced her hand to rise slowly toward his. Got to blend in. The nanobots on her hands would sanitize them—and his—anyway.

"Hey, dummy," said another, deeper voice. "Can't you tell Aimlee doesn't want to touch your hand?" She turned and faced the newcomer. Older. Taller. Broader through the shoulders. Faded jeans, plaid shirt, heavy boots. But the same angular planes to the face, the same hawk nose, the same mahogany hair hanging over one eye. Even from two meters away she could smell cedar shavings. A logger. "You'll have to forgive my little brother," he said. "Slow on the social cues."

"Hey!" protested Quin. But he dropped his hand, dug into his apron pocket, and produced his own mask.

"I'm Quill," said the newcomer. His mask hung below a dimpled, whisker shadowed, chin.

"Quill and Quin?" asked Aimlee. "Did your parents hate you?"

"Oh, it gets worse," laughed Quill. He pointed at his brother. "May I present Quinault Hoh Bridger." He laid his hand on his own chest. "And I'm Quillayute Calawah Bridger."

"What a mouthful!" said Aimlee. "Native American tribes and rivers around here?" The names were familiar, of course. Her drone swarms had carefully documented the entire Peninsula, its National Park, roads, towns, people, and animals in the past month. "Some sense of humor, your parents."

"You don't know the half of it," said Quill, grinning. "It's just such a beautiful part of the world, you can't help falling in love with it."

Aimlee nodded, looking up into his eyes. Brown with flecks of gold. "I know what you mean," she mumbled.

"Hey, I'd love to show you around, if you have any extra time," said Quill. "I mean, if you haven't seen everything already. Will you be here long?"

As a matter of fact, Aimlee thought, she had seen everything. She was sure her drones had captured things he would never see, even living here his entire life. "A couple more days," she said. "Then we head for home." Seeing this place through Quill's native eyes—those breathtaking brown eyes—would be a refreshing change. So would getting out of the bus and away from the rest of the research team, even if only for an hour or two.

"Great," he said, a dazzling smile making his dimpled chin dance. "I'll text you."

She held out her phone, an anachronistic piece of twenty-first-century camouflage. He tapped in his number and handed it back. As he did so his own phone chimed an incoming message. He glanced down and his eyebrows shot up. "That's a cool trick," he said. "How did you text me your number so quick? I didn't even see you do it."

Oh crap. She had reflexively flicked a command to the microscopic comms unit that floated in the corner of her eye. She grinned up at him. "I guess you haven't downloaded the newest updates yet."

He snorted and held up his phone. "This old piece of junk? Three models behind. Or is it four? Not the latest and greatest like yours." He shoved his phone in his pocket and pulled up his mask.

"And mine's his hand-me-down," said Quin, waving a phone with so many screen cracks Aimlee could barely tell it was a phone.

Quill turned to his brother. "Oh geez! I got distracted." He dropped a wink at Aimlee that caught at her breath. "Mom called and told me to come pick you up," he said to his brother. "There's a lot of crap going on in town tonight. She wants you straight home after work. I already put your bike in my truck. Go ask Jen if you can clock out a couple of minutes early."

The brothers turned toward the back of the store. Quill turned and walked backwards down the aisle. "Nice to meet you," he said. "I'll text."

"I hope you do," she said.

She paid for her groceries with the unfamiliar plastic card provided by the Smithsonian Time Travel office and strode out the door.

Suddenly she was in the glare of lights of dozens of large 4-wheel drive trucks. Unlike the few scattered cars when she had gone into the store, the parking lot now buzzed with activity. A steady stream of pickups, side-by-side SUVs, and dirt bikes dropped down from Main Street and swirled toward a single focal point: the fifty-year-old converted school bus that had been home and rolling VR holo production studio for Aimlee, her parents, and her grandmother for the last month. The ancient bus was ringed with vehicles, all pointed inward, the circle of headlights blazing from its chalky white paint.

Aimlee ran, weaving among the crowded vehicles. The pickup beds were full of camouflage-clad men lounging on hoods, standing in beds, leaning against roll bars. Everywhere assault weapons, hunting rifles, and shotguns pointed at the sky. Everyone she passed wore a handgun.

She burst through the inner circle of trucks and sprinted to the side of the bus, where the door folded inward to admit her. "What in the world is going on?" she panted, hurtling up the steps. None of the men outside had put out a hand to stop her from coming in. She assumed someone trying to get out would have been met quite differently.

"We have no idea," said her mother, Aiko. She crouched in the aisle and peered out the side window. "They started arriving just before you got back."

"What do they want?"

"Don't know," grunted her father from the driver's seat. He was the expedition's semi-official chauffeur. "But I'm glad you got back out here."

"Excuse me, dear," said Aimlee's grandmother, sidling past. "Rick, open the door for me, would you please?"

"Mother," said Aiko. "You're not going out there, are you?"

"Why yes, dear," said Nana, serene as a mountain lake. "Yes, I am. Rick, the door, please."

"Mother!" said Aiko, more insistently. "This is not the twenty-third century. You don't know how these people are going to react to a black woman."

"An elderly black woman," said Nana. "Remember your history, dear. I'm counting on the stereotypes of the day to protect me. None of those boys out there are going to see me as a threat."

Aiko thought about this. She gestured at her husband. "Nothing like how they would react to a white man, that's for sure."

"Or an athletic black woman like you, Mother," put in Aimlee.

"You don't see me moving a muscle," said Rick, his smile somehow simultaneously tense and wry. He kept his hands on the bus's large steering wheel, plainly visible to the men outside. "Aiko, you and I had better stay still. You too, Aimlee."

"The door, Rick," said Nana again.

"I'll get it," said Aimlee, pulling on the big silver crank and folding the door inward. She helped Nana down the three tall steps to the ground and stepped out after her.

"Aimlee!" There was a flare of panic at the edges of her mother's voice.

"It's alright, Mother," she said. "I'll just help Nana. We'll be right back. Get the door, would you please, Daddy?" She stared up into Rick's wide eyes and gave him a reassuring smile. "Right back. Promise." He looked as if he might vomit any second, but he pushed the door shut.

Aimlee popped open the canister in her pocket. She laid open her right palm, made the correct finger gestures, and the nanobots spread into the night sky, rapidly dispersing over the parking lot like a puff of vapor. Everything that happened here would be part of the VR record.

Nana led the way into the blaze of headlights in front of the bus, leaning on Aimlee's arm. "Help you boys with something?" Her voice was light and unstrained.

Beyond the lights there was a murmur of voices, then a silence.

"What the hell!" said a voice to their right. "Don't look like no Antifa to me."

"Just 'cause they don't look like Antifa don't mean

they're not," growled a low, gravelly voice directly ahead.

"I can assure you, gentlemen," said Nana, "that we are not Antifa."

"What's 'Antifa'?" Aimlee asked her grandmother, aloud for the surrounding militia to hear. She thought she must have ignored some vital piece of the pre-mission briefing, but Nana seemed to know what they were talking about. Aimlee realized she had tuned out the parts of the lecture that had dealt with the historical background of the mission. This year was certainly an inflection point in world history, even she remembered that, but she left those concerns to her parents and their colleagues. A time travel assignment to control swarms of camera drones large and small—now that was something to get excited about.

"Short for anti-fascists," said Nana, eyes boring into Aimlee's. "A loose group from the early twenty-first century who styled themselves as resistance fighters, believers in direct action. Arson. Vandalism."

Aimlee understood. Shut up and follow my lead. Gotcha, Nana. She nodded.

"That's right," said the gravelly voice beyond the lights. "Rioters. Anarchists. Ain't gonna happen in Tillicum. We protect our own."

"Yeah," said the voice from Aimlee's right. "The guy from the gun store over to Port Angeles sent us an email tonight warning that you were coming."

"Us?" asked Aimlee.

"You," replied the voice. "He warned us about you. Said a whole busload of Antifa was headed our way to burn Tillicum to the ground."

"You can relax, young man," said Nana. "We have nothing to do with any of that. My family and I have been camping in the National Park for almost a month."

"Doing what, exactly?" asked the gravelly voice.

"Relaxing. Taking lots of pictures," said Nana.

Millions and millions of pictures, thought Aimlee. Creating an immersive holographic VR of beauty that will soon no longer exist. But you all haven't realized yet that your way of life is dying.

"Really," she blurted. "We're not anti-fascists like those people. Or fascists like you gentlemen. Ouch! Nana! What did you do that for?" She yanked her arm away from her grandmother and rubbed at the deep fingernail marks Nana had left in her arm.

There was a loud, angry murmur. "What the hell did you just call us?" exclaimed the gravelly voice. Angry profanities came from every side.

Nana's soft voice rose over the din. "Please, gentlemen, excuse my granddaughter. She really knows nothing about politics. Or current events." Nana riveted Aimlee's eyes with hers. "Nothing." Aimlee's stomach sank. She had run her mouth when she should have stayed quiet.

"I'm sorry," she said. "Really, I didn't mean to offend you by calling you fascists."

Now the gravelly voice took on a shape. A burly man in fatigues, one of the largest men Aimlee had ever seen, cradling an assault rifle, stepped in front of the lights and advanced on the two women. All around the circle other men materialized, menacing in their silence.

"Maybe you're Antifa and maybe you're not," the big man said. "Guess we won't know until we search you. Open the door of the bus. We find any weapons, tactical gear, explosives, spray paint, anything . . . well, then we'll know, won't we?"

Aimlee exchanged glances with Nana. A search of the bus would turn up nothing of the sort, of course—all of that was strictly forbidden under the time transportation regulations—but there was an awful lot of tech on the bus that was going to be impossible to explain. Drones of various sizes, cutting edge tech even for Aimlee's own time. Batteries that would power a large twenty-first-century city. The quantum computers in the bus's VR editing suite that had more processing and storage than the combined capacity of all of twenty-first-century humanity's information technology combined—virtually unrecognizable to these people. The last thing the expedition could allow would be to have their tech fall into the hands of this century's scientists. The historical implications would be beyond comprehension.

Which is why, as Aimlee and Nana locked eyes in silent understanding, they knew that the expedition hung on a knife's edge. Before he could allow their gear to be seized, before any of these gunmen could force his way onto the bus, Rick would have no choice but to trigger the self-destruct command that would turn all their tech into piles of melted plastic and silicon.

Most catastrophic of all, worse even than a month of lost VR recordings, would be the loss of the jump computer. If that happened, Aimlee, her parents, and her grandmother would be stranded. Marooned in time.

The big man stepped toward the bus.

"Hey hey hey!" A voice rang out from beyond the circle of headlights. A peculiar rattling clatter came closer and closer, louder and louder. Before Aimlee could identify the sound, two heavily-loaded shopping carts, one with a wobbling wheel, hurtled at high speed into the lit circle and skidded to a stop. "It looks like we're just in time! Hey Jerry. Hey Aimlee."

"What the . . ." exclaimed the big man. "Bridger, what are you doing here?"

"Sorry, Jer," said Quill, grinning ear to ear. "We're a little late with the refreshments. Aren't we, Quin?" He began lifting cold cases of Michelob out of his shopping cart, gesturing to his brother to do the same, and set them on the hoods of each of the surrounding pickups. He walked his last case directly to Nana and handed it to her.

He dropped a wink at Aimlee. "Compliments of Aimlee's dad." He waved at Rick, staring open-mouthed from the driver's seat of the bus. "Drink up!"

"What the hell, Bridger?" spat Jerry.

"I see you've met my friends from Spokane," said Quill. "No Antifa here. Aimlee's family came to party. They said we should invite a few of my friends, too." He twisted off a cap and thrust the bottle into Jerry's fist. "They're going to park their bus out at my mom's tonight." He arched his eyebrows at Aimlee and Nana. "In fact, why don't you guys go park the bus? Quin will bring you back in my truck. Let's all meet at the pavilion in Tillicum Park. Twenty minutes? Great!" He slapped Jerry on the back and made a circling motion in the air. "Head 'em up, move 'em out, guys!" he yelled.

Jerry shrugged, waved his arm. Around the circle cases of beer were retrieved from hoods, doors slammed, engines rumbled.

Quill offered Nana one arm, Aimlee the other, and walked them toward the bus, whose motor was coughing to life. "Head straight north," he said under the rumble of vertical exhausts and crunch of oversized tires, his easy smile in marked contrast with his urgent words. "Go straight past the park. My mom's house is just beyond it, but you keep going. Just follow the highway. Don't stop until you're off the Peninsula."

He held Nana's elbow as she climbed the steps of the bus, then turned to leave. Aimlee laid her hand on his arm. "I don't know why you stuck your neck out like that, but believe me, I could not be more grateful."

He looked deeply into her eyes, then Nana's. "Tell you the truth, I'm just playing a hunch. I don't think you and your family are a bunch of rioters. I hope I'm not wrong."

"You're not wrong," she said. "My parents are academics. There's nothing political about any of us."

He nodded, satisfied. "I've lived here all my life, and I've never seen folks this scared. They feel like they have to protect their homes and families."

"Of course they do," said Nana.

"I couldn't just let them treat you like violent enemies," Quill said. "No telling what some hothead would have done once they got to tearing your bus apart."

"That would have been scary," said Aimlee. And catastrophic. The family would have been stuck here forever.

"Just do us and yourselves all a favor and just get as far away from here as you can," Quill said. He smiled and held her eyes for a long moment. "But do come back in a few months when things have settled down. I would really like to get to know you." He held her hand as she climbed into the bus, and stepped back as the door closed and the engine belched and revved. A few months, huh? thought Aimlee. If only. His optimism was so charming and tragic that her breath caught in her throat.

As her drone swarm gathered, she watched Nana lean

out the window of the bus, tap Quill on the shoulder, and drop a neatly strapped bundle of crisp new $100 banknotes into his startled hands. "For all that beer," she said. "I don't know how much it was, but I hope this covers it."

Rick ground the transmission into gear and pulled up onto the highway, leaving Quill staring wide-eyed at the bundle of cash.

Nana leaned over Rick's shoulder, navigating according to Quill's instructions. As the bus rattled north along Highway 101, Aimlee watched a long line of trucks, SUVs, and motorcycles stream out of the parking lot and form into a procession behind them. Beyond the center of town, they passed Tillicum Park, and the procession peeled away.

They rode in tense silence for several minutes, watching unbroken walls of cedars pass on both sides of the highway. Nana pointed at the old analog needle waver around 50. "What does that mean?" she asked. "How fast are we going?"

"Miles per hour," replied her son-in-law. "About 80 kph."

"Practically crawling," said Aimlee.

"Can't you go any faster?" asked Nana.

"I'm pushing it as it is," answered Rick. "We chose this bus for camouflage, to blend in with the working-class communities around here, not for speed."

"Internal combustion," sighed Nana. "Collector's item. Never meant to run from a mob."

"Exactly," said Rick. "Next time we'll—" As he spoke there was a loud bang. A cloud of steam enveloped the front of the bus and rusty water streamed across the windshield. "That's not good."

"But the engine is still running?" asked Aiko.

"Yeah, but the temperature gauge is rising," he said, tapping a small dial on the dash panel. "Gotta get off the road before it burns itself up."

Peering through the cloud of steam into the twin cones of the bus's headlights, Aimlee pointed at a break in the trees. "Is that a road?"

"Not much of one," said Rick. "But we really don't have much choice." Brakes squealed and protested, he wrestled the huge steering wheel, and he bounced into the ruts of what Aimlee recognized from their mapping expedition as an old logging road. The branches of young, thick trees brushed both sides of the bus. The track ahead was a tunnel of night-black, close-packed conifers.

"I've got us on GPS," said Aiko. "You have less than a kilometer before this road ends at the Sol Duc River."

"Any place to turn around?" asked Rick. The antique motor coughed, then surged. "Never mind. Engine is about to seize."

"What does that mean?" asked Aimlee.

"It means this old tub has had it," said Rick. He nursed the accelerator, trying to keep the bus moving ahead. "Aimlee, get a drone swarm up. We need to know what's around us."

She surged into action, throwing open the back door of the bus and cranking open several large skylights. Streams of silent drones of various sizes flowed up and out into the night, spreading above the trees.

"There's the river," said Rick, bringing the bus to a grinding stop and turning off the engine. The lights died. Hisses of steam, gurgles, and popping of cooling metal echoed in the darkness. As the sounds of the engine faded, Aimlee could hear the burbles of the river only a few meters away.

"Holo," she commanded. A display sprang into being, glowing the muted tones of night-vision: the bus, the logging road, the river, the highway, as seen from fifty meters above.

"Uh oh," said Nana, pointing at the display. Two pickup trucks had pulled off the highway at the entrance to the logging road and four men were getting out. "Not good. Can you get me audio?"

"Almost there," said Aimlee, concentrating on her controls. A detachment of bots, silent as night birds, circled in on the four men until their faces and voices were distinct in the holo.

"Told ya I saw them pull off. Boiled over," the big man with the gravelly voice said, kneeling next to a puddle of radiator fluid at the edge of the asphalt.

"Rusted-out old piece of crap," laughed another man. "Trust Antifa to come all the way out here in a bucket of bolts that should never have left Seattle."

"Well, we've got them where we want them," growled Jerry. "Shall we have some fun?" He hurled a Michelob bottle into the long grass at the side of the highway, then reached into the bed of his truck.

"What's that he's got?" asked Aiko.

Aimlee peered at the holo. "It looks like one of those noisy things the loggers use to cut down the trees."

"Chain saw," supplied Nana, her voice grim. "Big one." On the holo, the other man soon had his own saw, and the group made their way on foot a hundred meters down the tree-lined logging road, headlamps boring holes in the darkness.

"These'll do," said Jerry, eyeing a pair of trees on

either side of the road. The saws roared to life. With professional ease the four men felled a pair of trees with trunks as big around as Aimlee's waist, dropping them directly across the road. There was now no way for the bus to get back to the highway, even if the engine were somehow miraculously restored to life.

"Now what do we do?" Aimlee asked.

"We see what their intentions are," said Nana. "Let's hope they'll be satisfied with blocking us in and will just go away and leave us alone."

"Something tells me that's not going to happen," said Rick. "Look."

The four men had returned to the trucks at the side of the highway, ditched the saws, and came away with night vision goggles, and assault rifles with infrared scopes. One pair went through the trees to the left of the logging road, the other to the right.

Rick sighed. "Well, I guess that just about makes up our minds for us," he said. "We have to go home. What do you think, Aiko? How long until we can jump?"

"Too long," said Aiko, "if they're really intent on killing us. The return function on the jump computer is set for a precise picosecond two days from now. I'll have to recalculate the whole thing."

"Can't we just jump?" asked Nana. "What's a couple of days of time slip among friends?"

"It's more than just time," frowned Aiko. "The universe is moving. The Milky Way is moving. The sun and the earth are both moving. If we just make the time jump, without recalculating and compensating for all the orbital movements, we'll most likely jump to empty space."

"If we're lucky," muttered Aimlee.

"If we're lucky," agreed Aiko. "The fastest I've ever done a full calc is twenty minutes. And that's with a pre-set departure time. I have to set that as a given before I start to calculate."

"So we jump twenty minutes from now?" said Rick.

"On it," said Aiko, and locked her concentration on the jump computer. "Here's your countdown." She swiped a slave display of the clock into the holo so that it glowed near the ceiling. She glanced up at Rick. "You've got your finger on the self-destruct, don't you?"

"I do," he nodded grimly. "But be ready to move quickly. If a gunshot stops my heart, in three seconds the self-destruct will happen automatically."

"More company," announced Nana, pointing at the display. Another pickup had joined the first pair. "Who are they? They look familiar."

"That," said Aimlee, bending to look closely, "is Quill and his little brother Quin."

"The beer boys?" asked Nana. "What are they doing here?"

Aimlee shifted uncomfortably. "I . . . um . . . I texted that we had car trouble. Gave him our location."

In Aimlee's display, Quill and Quin had made their way from the highway to the fallen trees. "Start cutting and clearing," Quill told his brother. "I'll see if I can't go talk some sense into those guys." He trotted into the dark down the narrow logging road.

Minutes ticked away as Aimlee watched the four loggers creep through the woods along either side of the logging road. She hardly dared breathe. Behind them, Quill, without the advantage of night vision goggles in the moonless, tree-shrouded darkness of the forest, struggled slowly along the rutted track.

He had only covered half the distance from the highway to the bus when the armed men came close enough to catch sight of the bus. They dropped prone to train their night vision scopes on the bus. Through the windows, red laser dots wavered and settled on her parents and her grandmother.

She could wait no longer. The fingers of her right hand scribbled the palm of her left. The closest of the four men lifted suddenly into the air. He screamed, reflexively squeezed the trigger of his AR, which chattered and flew from his hands. He somersaulted forward, dodging and swerving through the trees and out over the river. He cartwheeled through the air and landed with a mighty splash.

"Aimlee Janes-Whoden! You know it's not safe to use drones to pick up human beings," scolded her father. "How fast can you do it again?"

The other three men, startled by the scream and the errant shots, opened fire. "Get down!" yelled Rick. Wild shots pinged off the heavy steel sides of the ancient bus. Glass shattered.

Aimlee found herself on the floor, staring up into the display, fingers flying. A cloud of tiny drones coalesced around another of the prone, camouflaged men, and he lifted from the ground, screaming. He followed his companion into the river.

Jerry and the remaining man, on the opposite side of the road and the bus, fired wildly into the darkness. Aimlee chose the smaller of the two as her next target. The cloud formed around him, then he too screamed as he was hurled into the darkness.

Aimlee saw Jerry take his eyes from his night vision scope and sprint toward the road, head down. Quill, charging blindly toward the gunfire, clearly did not see him coming and was thrown from his feet. He fell, stunned. Jerry rose, dragging the unresisting boy by the collar. He dropped his AR, pulled a .45, and jammed it in Quill's mouth.

"Enough!" he bellowed. "I don't know what you did to my friends, but I've got your little buddy. Don't make me kill him!"

Aimlee froze. Her hands were shaking so hard she could hardly issue commands. She glanced up at the countdown clock. Six minutes.

Quill groaned, stirred, slowly regaining consciousness. Without hesitation, Jerry jerked the .45 from his mouth and clipped his temple with it. Quill's head lolled.

Aimlee struck. Her fingers splayed and drones zeroed in.

Jerry screamed as the first drones hit his eyes, then choked to silence as writhing masses of winged metal machines stuffed themselves into his mouth and throat. His trigger finger clutched spasmodically, and he emptied his magazine into the air. He dropped his gun and fell, clawing at his mouth and eyes, fighting to breathe.

Aimlee leaped from the bus and ran to stand over his struggling form. She stared down, fingers poised to recall the drones that were choking him. But should she? He had targeted her family. He had attacked Quill and threatened to kill him. Who would blame her if she just let him choke to death?

She felt a hand on her shoulder. "Here. I'll help you," said Nana. She held out a roll of strong tape. Aimlee hesitated, then nodded. Together they dragged the struggling logger against a tree and bound him. Only then did Aimlee disperse the drones and allow him to drag in a gasping breath.

Two minutes later she knelt over Quill as he slowly regained consciousness. Her comms system signaled that both sets of nanosurgeons, those that had repaired his torn scalp, and those working on his concussed brain, had returned to the bus's first aid kit. Those achingly beautiful brown eyes fluttered open, and he reached up to touch her, as if to make sure she was real. She gave his hand a reassuring squeeze.

"You're going to be fine," she said, rising to her feet. "I have to go. I'm going to have to leave it to you how to explain what happened to this guy." She jerked her chin at Jerry, who glowered at them around a duct tape gag. From the direction of the highway, she could hear sirens.

"But," sputtered Quill, struggling to sit up. "What did happen? I have no idea. I just heard shooting and came to help. That's the last I remember."

"I can't believe you came running," said Aimlee. She bent and kissed him lightly on the cheek. "You're a heck of a guy."

"Aimlee, twenty seconds," said Nana from the door of the bus.

She kissed him again, this time full on the lips. "Goodbye," she said.

"You coming back when all this is over?"

She climbed the steps, turned, tears streaking her face. "I'll try," she said, knowing full well it could never be. She had already looked him up. He had survived Covid-19 but had died with his entire family early in the Second Civil War.

She closed the door, held up a trembling hand, and the bus was empty.

Scott E. Tarbet

Scott Tarbet's speculative fiction stories have garnered multiple awards, critical acclaim, and entertain a burgeoning fanbase. He writes in several genres, including Steampunk, fantasy, paranormal, techno-thriller, and historical fiction.

When he is not submerged in one of his created worlds, which he finds nearly as fascinating as the real one, he sings opera profession-ally and slow-smokes thousands of pounds of authentic Texas-style barbeque. He was married in full Elizabethan regalia, loves Ste-ampunk and cosplay conventions of all flavors. He makes his home in the mountains of Utah.

Bag Lady

by Gail Boling

"So, you the bag lady?"

The voice is husky, edged with fatigue. The hoodie covers half her weathered face. She stands to the side of the line for food.

"I am," I reply, hoping to sound optimistic.

"We camp outside the library." A distinct odor emanates from her. Fire smoke and unwashed clothing. Does she even own a toothbrush?

"How many of you are there?" I have less than a dozen mats made up.

"We come and go."

"So, how many mats do you need?"

"How many you got?"

"Why don't I show you one and you can decide if it will work for you?"

"Sure. I just don't want to lose my place in line for the food."

"Go ahead. You can come back when you're through the line."

She shuffles back into line, the empty backpack hanging low over her shoulders.

The line trails out into the crisp autumn air—all ages, all races, all hungry. The food bank volunteers sort the canned goods and perishables into prearranged piles, bagging them for the clients. The regulars make special requests.

"Can I have spaghetti instead of potatoes?"

"Do you have any bread?"

"I need bottled water. Got any?"

The volunteers try not to look bothered. The regular staff works in the back, breaking down boxes and shelving the goods.

I wonder what I am even doing here and swat that thought away.

The bag lady.

My crochet circle has taken up making "plarn" from strips of plastic shopping bags and crocheting it into sleeping mats for the homeless. This is a big trend on the internet. Kill two birds with one stone. Recycle plastic and provide aid to the homeless at the same time. Win-win, right?

I sure hope so.

She comes back with a male friend, her backpack bulging heavier now.

"This the bag lady. She going to help us out."

The eyes are analyzing, reserved, bloodshot.

I don't want to make a big scene out of this. So I take them to the side and unwrap a mat. It's brown and white: Smith's and Harmons. It took Cassie half a week to crochet, and she's fast.

"That it?" She looks skeptical. She glances at her friend, shaking her head. "It looks like a giant grocery sack."

Well, that's actually what it is.

"How it supposed to keep the water out with all those little holes?"

"It's not exactly waterproof," I begin.

The friend grunts in exasperation.

"But it's lightweight and soft and will keep you off the ground."

"Lady, have you tried sleeping on one of these?" She picks up the mat, stretching it out of shape. "What you trying to say? We garbage? This all we deserve?"

I'm glad Cassie is not here to see this.

"We're just trying to help you."

"Help." She practically spits the word out. "Help is all we get. We don't need your kind of help."

"I'm confused," I say. "I thought you wanted help."

"Not this way."

The friend speaks up. "Don't listen to Lonnie. She's the angry one. I like your mats. Got any more?"

I pull out a few more. They're all basically the same. They took hours of work. I wonder if anyone will even use them.

"Where is your camp?" I try to sound interested.

"We outside the library."

I try not to imagine what goes on in the library bathrooms.

"Even in the winter?"

"All the time. You want to stop by?"

That thought had never occurred to me.

"Sure."

"Like right now?"

"Well, I'm not sure right now."

"What are you afraid of?" She challenges me again. "We don't have fleas."

I wonder if humans can get fleas.

"Okay," I hear myself saying. "Let me get my stuff."

We walk the seven blocks to the library.

The sky turns an angry orange that fades. The yellow-ish streetlamps compete with the soft moonlight.

The camp, stretched out on a parking strip trampled bare of grass, is an assortment of tents, shopping carts, bicycles, tarpaulin stretched over frames, a couple of dogs on leashes, cardboard boxes, and garbage. A small fire burns.

They stand on the outskirts and wait for me to say something.

I have driven by it many times before but never stopped.

I wonder where the drugs are, if there are knives or even guns.

I know that many of the homeless don't want to enter the shelters because they are afraid of crime. They feel safer on the streets.

I don't feel safer.

"Where do you sleep?" I ask.

She points down the narrow row of tents pitched curbside. She shrugs the backpack off her shoulders and onto the sidewalk.

The friend explains. "Lonnie and her man, they long-timers. They been here practically from the begin-ning."

No wonder she's angry. I wonder how they ended up here.

"Over five years," she says.

The winters are brutal. How in the world do they survive?

"You really stay on the streets in the winter?"

"We manage. Somehow."

Why? If you can survive winter on the streets, you can survive anything. Why do this to yourselves?

An argument breaks out around the campfire at the end of the row of tents. Voices are raised. People stand up and a man pushes a woman back to the ground.

"God damn it, Cody, why don't you just listen to her?"

"I swear I'll cut you if you do that again."

A woman's voice, pleading. "I didn't touch your stash. I don't even know where it is."

The sound of a hit, and the woman's voice crying now, choking.

"Jesus fucking Christ, Cody. I think you just knocked her tooth out."

Lonnie is already in the middle of this scene. She grabs the man by the hair and forces him to look at her. "Cody, I swear to God we going to kick you out of this camp if you don't stop beating on the women."

"Says you and which army?" He gives her an ugly grin.

"Don't start with me."

Agreement from the group. "Yeah, Cody, don't start with her."

"She's the senior now."

"She in charge."

Cody sits back down on the milk crate, glaring. "None of you better get in my stash, that's all I'm saying."

Lonnie looks at the woman cradling her jaw in her hands. "You bad, Sheila?"

Sheila spits blood. "It was loose already. He knocked it out."

"We best get some alcohol on that. I got some Wild Turkey in my tent. You come with me, now."

Sheila struggles to her feet, following Lonnie away from the fire and back towards us.

I am thinking this would be an excellent time for me

to leave.

"Can I just give you all the sleeping mats I have?" I ask Lonnie's friend.

"Sure thing. We'll find some use for them."

I pull them out of my tote bags, piling them on top of each other on the ground.

Lonnie is back with Sheila in tow.

"You leaving us already, Bag Lady?"

"I think so." I wonder how long it would take an Uber to get here.

"You seen enough?"

"I think so."

"You don't ever want to be out here, do you?"

"No, I don't think so."

Sheila spits out more blood, coughing.

"We need to get her to a doctor," I hear myself say. "Or a dentist."

"Ain't no dentist at the ER."

"Okay. But she still needs to be seen by somebody."

"You got a phone?"

"Yes."

"Call the paramedics."

The friend points to the stack of mats, and Sheila sits down on them, a trickle of blood running down her chin. I dig in my purse for some clean tissues and hand them to her. "No police," she says through puffed lips.

I dial 911.

"911, what's your emergency?"

"Well, it's not for me. It's for a homeless woman here at the encampment near the library. She just got a tooth knocked out."

"The police will be on their way."

"We are actually calling for the paramedics, not the

police."

"How did she get her tooth knocked out?"

"It was an accident." I pause. "She fell."

Sheila nods. Lonnie stands by, studying me. I can see Cody in the background, slinking away from the campsite.

The voice on the phone asks for my name and phone number.

"We'll send a paramedic unit from the fire department," she says.

"Thank you."

I look around. Several more people are standing up and walking away from the campsite, including everyone from around the campfire where Cody hit Sheila.

Lonnie mutters to herself. The friend drifts away to feed one of the dogs. Sheila dabs her lip and rocks slightly back and forth. A night breeze is picking up, bringing a slight chill to the air.

It doesn't take long for the paramedics to arrive. The gleaming boxy red truck pulls up and two EMTs step out, a man and a woman, both pulling on protective gloves. The woman grabs a kit.

"Hello, Lonnie," the tall one booms.

"Hello, Mort. Hello, Esperanza."

"What have we got here?"

Lonnie points. "Sheila here hurt herself. She banged up pretty bad in her mouth."

"Let's take a look. You know the drill. We have to take vitals first."

Sheila and Lonnie nod.

The EMTs kneel on the ground, shining a flashlight, recording vitals, and cleaning Sheila's mouth.

Sheila winces when the alcohol is applied.

"Do you have the tooth?"

Sheila hands over a bloody tissue.

"A dentist might be able to save this tooth if the bone around it is not fractured."

Sheila says nothing.

"You know the homeless clinic has a small dental practice. You might be able to get moved up the waiting list since this is an emergency."

Sheila looks at the ground.

"How did this happen?"

Sheila frowns. "I fell."

"Fell, how?" Esperanza's voice is kind but firm.

"You know, I tripped over a dog leash and fell."

"You've been doing a lot of tripping and falling lately, Sheila. You sure you're feeling okay?"

"As okay as I can."

"Wouldn't you be safer in the shelter?" Esperanza presses on. "You know we have to report if somebody is abusing you."

"Nobody."

I look hard at Lonnie, who stands silent in the background.

Esperanza sees my look. "You look new here," she says to me. "Did you see anything?"

Shit. I am not prepared for this.

"I was just dropping off some sleeping mats," I stammer. "I was just getting ready to leave."

"Did you see anything?" Esperanza stands up, all four feet ten of her, and looks me straight in the eye.

If not now, when?

"Yes, I did," I hear myself say. "Somebody named Cody took a swipe at her."

Sheila groans. Lonnie spits on the ground.

"Sheila, you know we got to write this up."

"I don't want no police."

"Whether you want it or not, that Cody has got to be stopped." Esperanza looks at Mort, who walks over to the truck radio and begins calling in a preliminary report.

"God damn it," Sheila mutters over and over.

"Your brother is out of control," Esperanza says patiently. "It's about time we put a stop to his violence."

By the time the police arrive, the encampment is completely deserted except for Lonnie, Sheila, me, and the EMTs. Even the dogs are gone. Just the tents shiver in the wind.

They take my statement. Lonnie and Sheila refuse to give one.

Esperanza and Mort take one more careful look at Sheila's mouth and bottle her tooth in a vial.

When the police and paramedics are gone, Lonnie hands me a tattered business card: J. Finlay, Volunteers of America, with a phone number and email.

"This the person you want to talk to if you really want to help, Bag Lady."

I nod.

I pull out my phone and order an Uber.

It is well past time to get out of here.

Later that night, at home in my living room with the kids long in bed, I nurse my glass of wine and thank my lucky stars for my humdrum middle-class life. My husband watches the recorded football game, swearing at the players.

I look at my bags of plarn. I think of the money I

have budgeted for fireworks next year for the Fourth of July—my birthday present to myself. I pull out the business card Lonnie gave me. Fireworks can wait. It's time to do something selfless.

I send my email, signed The Bag Lady.

Gail Boling

Definitely a bookmonger in a former life. Currently misshelved in a law firm. Waiting for that golden lottery ticket or retirement, whichever comes first, to start reading her way through the libraries.

Conviction

by Daniel Yocom

T he edge of the leaflet stung Tina when Velma pulled it out of her hand.

"You're not thinking." Velma threw the paper into the stove's firebox. "Can you imagine what would happen to Papa, and us, if you get involved in something like that?"

Tina sucked on the cut between her thumb and index finger as Velma assumed her "I'm your older sister" stance—head tilted, eyes narrowed, hands on hips, just enough movement so her dress swayed side-to-side.

"Velma, you know me better than that." Tina needed to remain calm. She and Velma talked through practically everything.

"If you're even considering this, it's clear you haven't been thinking."

The wagging finger was out. Probably a new record for that happening. Tina tried to tell Velma how important this was for both of them. But Velma was warmed up and spoke right over her words.

"Papa gets passed over for good-paying jobs already because of our past and how Mama died. If you start throwing more bricks, things will break. Do you want to stop him from getting work at all? Did you think about that? Furthermore, . . ."

Tina settled back and sipped her coffee. There wasn't going to be a conversation this morning.

". . . how do you think you and I would be treated by the people of this city? All you'd be doing is stirring up more trouble we don't need. What would Mama say if she was here?" Velma drew in a breath.

"From what you and Papa have said, I think Mama would be proud." Tina kept eye contact over the rim of her mug.

Velma stopped. Her mouth was open, then closed in a pucker as she stared down at Tina over the small dining room table. Her long braid of brown hair slid over her shoulder until it hung in front of her. Tina braced herself for the explosion building up. Velma wasn't stupid and she didn't like politics. Tina hoped her sister could help her, maybe just by listening for a change. Velma opened and closed her mouth a couple of times without saying anything. Maybe she was right. Maybe it was too dangerous to get involved in something new with all of the other things going on in St. Louis.

A door behind Tina creaked. There were three doors on that side of the apartment: the entrance—nobody had walked up the stairs, her and Velma's bedroom, and her father's room.

Velma smiled. "Papa, your breakfast is ready and your lunch is packed. I need to get to work. And, your youngest is insufferable." She grabbed her hat and shawl and was out of the apartment before another word could be spoken.

"Did Velma make your coffee?"

"No, Papa. I don't think she'll ever make me coffee again in this lifetime. We just had a difference of opinion about current events." Tina picked up a ribbon from the table and used it to busy herself by tying back her unruly red hair.

Sam picked up his bowl of oatmeal and started eating over the stove. "Were you trying to get a rise out of your sister this morning?" He took a bite and kept his eyes on Tina's.

"No, I had a serious question I wanted to discuss with her. Is everything all right, Papa? Why aren't you sitting?"

"I have to hurry." He set the bowl down and checked his pocket watch. "I have the opportunity to work on the façade of that estate being built for one of the railwaymen moving here from the east. With all those fools running after gold in California, the Guild's been left shorthanded."

"You didn't say anything about this last night." Tina got up and cleared the table.

"No, I didn't. Velma likes to get overly hopeful. I don't know how long I'll be allowed to work on this job. Lud got me on the list late yesterday. I might not be there a second day when the Guild's foreman sees me on site. But I'll get at least one good day's pay because he won't dare cut me in front of everyone unless I give him a reason. What were you asking Velma about?" He filled his mouth with food.

"Oh, I was expressing concerns about my place in society."

"Society, or the household?" Another spoonful.

"Oh, no, Papa. It was not about anything in our home." Tina blew out the lamp on the table. The glow from the firebox and the early dawn allowed her to see the room but put her face in shadow.

"I hope you weren't just getting your sister riled up."

He set his spoon in the empty bowl and picked up his lunch bucket. "The two of you have different views on life, almost like night and day. You always have. And I expect you always will. She wants to keep everything calm without anyone taking much notice of her."

"I know, Papa. I really did want to know what she thought because of just that reason. She made her thoughts clear. 'Women, like children, should be seen and not heard.' Anyway, you said you need to get going. I'm going to the diner and see if they will let me start early. If not, I'll beg on the corner until I can wait the tables."

"Not funny, young lady."

Tina left the diner when the sun was halfway down the western sky. Serving lunch never made as much money as breakfast. But today she earned a couple of extra hours of tips to buy some vegetables. Hoping it wasn't too late to get some, she headed toward the warehouse where teamsters unloaded the wagons from the local farms.

Tina held her hair and shawl over her nose as she approached. There was no wind, and the smells of the Mississippi and the rotting vegetables culled from that morning's deliveries combined to create an extraordinary stench.

Mrs. Abernathy smiled and waved at Tina. She sat on one crate while rummaging through another. "How's your pa, doing? I was hoping you might stop by this afternoon. This morning saw a load come in from someone's cold storage. Had to do a lot of sorting. I've been cleaning up what I can since then. I have a couple of heads of cabbage and some potatoes I've set aside for you."

"Thank you, Mrs. Abernathy. And we are all doing well. I'll let Papa know you asked about him, again."

The older woman blushed. "He's a good man, and he shouldn't have to raise you girls on his own."

"Yes, he is." Tina handed over some coins and put the vegetables in her basket. "This will be enough to make soup for a couple of nights. Thank you for what you do." She bent closer. "It's because of strong women like you that give me strength and belief in making things better."

Mrs. Abernathy put her hand on Tina's shoulder and kissed her cheek. "Ah, Tina, we just need to work together to make life better. Thank you for the kind words. Now, go make your pa some good hearty soup."

The evening breeze picked up and blew the odors out over the river. Tina settled her shawl back onto her shoulders and breathed in the fresh air as she walked home.

Ahead, a crowd listened to a man talking and gesturing from atop a large crate. Another man stood below him and handed out flyers to anyone who would take one. More people were joining the group as Tina neared the corner.

He was preaching abolitionism.

They had different faces but spoke the same message. The crowd was only white folks. There were no colored people among the listeners. Men had decided Missouri could join the Union as a slave state—which was a load of pig manure—and anyone in this crowd was putting their lives in danger, especially if they weren't white.

She didn't need to hear what the speakers said; she'd already read several fliers. Still, she moved around the edge of the crowd as she passed to hear if there was something new.

Somebody threw something at the orator. People started cursing and a brawl broke out. Tina picked up her pace toward the other side of the street before the fighting could spread to the back of the gathering.

Men fought with fists or whatever they held. Some went to the ground and kept fighting from there. Papa and Lud talked about prizefighters on the riverboats and how they had rules, but nobody was following any here. She turned away, not wanting to see people get hurt.

Whistles blew as policemen rushed the area. They arrived so fast and in such numbers, they must have been standing ready and waiting for things to turn violent. Officers with clubs moved into the fray while others stood back and yelled at the men rolling in the street. They even brought a wagon.

Brawlers fled in all directions. The police let most of them get away and focused their efforts on those who were closest to where the abolitionist had been speaking and the fighting looked to be the fiercest.

This was how people treated each other over ideas. It didn't matter if there was a right or wrong, it became us versus them. At least the women weren't part of the fighting. Though some were on the sides of the ruckus cheering and yelling.

Two men pushed each other as they ran towards Tina. Off-balance, one stumbled into her and knocked her down. She snatched at her basket as a head of cabbage bounced out.

A black boot stopped the cabbage from rolling away. The officer squatted and picked it up. He barely glanced at the vegetable as he watched his fellow officers wrangling up the combatants.

"You're lucky, miss, that you weren't in the middle of that mob. It might've been more than a cabbage head rolling."

He smiled, probably proud of himself for the dark humor he thought up so quickly. Tina stood, gathered the potatoes, put them back in her basket, and took the cabbage the man had picked up.

"Thank you, officer. I was just passing when the commotion broke out."

"That's good you weren't involved. These abolitionists are becoming more and more dangerous. They just keep making trouble for all the decent folks. They should just leave or accept the natural order to things."

"So, you agree that holding another man's life as property is a natural thing?" Tina was looking down as she brushed dirt from her dress.

"Let me just say, people who go about telling others to change their ways and aren't the proper authority are going to be dealt with by the law. The law in Missouri is it's legal. We are charged with upholding and enforcing the law to protect honest people who abide by the law. Now, it's best if you just move along and let us do our job, without interference."

The officer glared at Tina and bounced his club into his open palm.

Tina clenched her jaw and forced a pleasant smile. "I'm sorry, officer. I meant no offense. I just get curious and ask questions. Sometimes speaking before my womanly brain considers what I'm saying or how I'm saying it. I'm on my way. And, again, thank you for rescuing my cabbage."

She turned to a side street and stepped away.

Tina set the table for two. The kerosene lamp lit the table, and its aroma mixed with the soup she stirred on the stove. The creak of the stairs in the hallway outside the apartment made Tina smile. Even with all the other noises in the tenement, she could always hear that step. And she knew it was Papa that made it creak that way.

He was covered in sweat and dirt from a long day of work. He smiled broadly at Tina as he put his lunch pail on the counter.

Tina greeted him while pouring hot water into the washbasin. "Dinner is ready, as soon as you're cleaned up."

"Thank you, my dear. I take it Velma has already left for her dinner with John's family."

"Yes, she thinks they should be able to open a bakery within the year. She really is a better baker than him. Anyway, she's all excited because she believes they are going to be discussing wedding plans." She spun towards her father with a loaf of bread held up between them. "And, don't start on me about my future." She continued her spin to lay the bread on the table.

"Trust me, I don't have the energy to get into that discussion tonight." He smiled and finished washing his face and hands. "The soup smells wonderful. Let me guess. Cabbage, and potatoes?"

Tina placed the bowls on the table. "Oh, Papa, you have an absolutely amazing sense of deduction."

He sat and cut the bread. "Now, I think you should tell me what happened today. I can tell there is a story to be told."

"What do you mean?"

"The backside of your dress is dirty. It looks like you were sitting in the gutter. I hope you weren't begging for the potatoes."

"Oh, I was knocked down in the street."

"What?" The knife stopped in mid-stroke.

"Nothing to be concerned about, Papa. Men were running from the police, and I didn't get out of the way fast enough."

He didn't move.

"That didn't come out right. I was walking past a corner where an abolitionist was speaking. A fight broke out. The police were there, immediately, and the brawlers ran in all directions. Before I could get out of the way, two of them knocked into me and I found myself sitting in the street. Luckily for me, an officer was standing nearby and made sure no one else ran me over. He also rescued one of the heads of cabbage as it was also trying to make a break for it." Tina sipped her soup.

"By God, daughter. You never cease to amaze me how you end up in the middle of some of the strangest events. I don't think you are attracted to mischief, but mischief is attracted to you."

They ate in silence for a couple of minutes.

"An abolitionist was speaking on a corner? And you happened to be there?"

"Yes. Oh, and the widow Abernathy asked how you're doing." Tina smiled sweetly.

"Now, don't you start on that topic. She always smells of soured vegetables. And, yes, I know she is a good person. But I get the feeling you are trying to change the subject."

"I really was passing by on my way home after buying the vegetables."

"Does this abolitionist have anything to do with what you were talking to your sister about this morning?" He took a big bite of bread. He always seemed to get inquisitive when they were eating and used chewing his food to leave questions hanging in the air.

Tina set her spoon down.

"Not directly. Papa, is it wrong to try to make the world a better place, for everyone? I mean, there are a lot of unfair rules and laws out there. Our family is living proof of that. I just don't know what I should do sometimes. The abolitionists are working to change one imbalance." Tina looked down at her hands on either side of her bowl.

"Tina, the world isn't all wrong. But it can be scary. There are people willing to hurt, even kill, others who don't agree with them. You have to be careful about the risks you take. The abolitionists are playing a very dangerous game." His hand reached out until their fingers were touching.

"I know they are. That's something I feel strongly about, but I don't know if I like their methods—the fighting keeps getting worse. Maybe in a free state I would feel safe enough to do something. But here, for me, for us, it's too dangerous."

"That's what's been troubling you then?"

She looked up at his narrowed brow and soft, searching eyes. She knew the struggles he'd faced when he married a woman from a family of higher society. And how it got worse when she was killed in an accident on a site he was working on. Tina didn't want to bring more trouble.

"Talk with me, Tina. Tell me what is bothering you?"

"Papa, I don't want to cause you or Velma more problems."

"Oh, daughter. Trust me, I create enough of my own.

I can tell this is troubling you deeply. So, let me remind you that you have been raised to be smart. It's what your mother and I both wanted. She said it would give you girls better opportunities, better chances, if you knew how to read and to think for yourselves. I agreed with her then, as I still do."

"But what if I do something that makes it harder for you to get work?" Tina's vision was a little blurry as she fought to control her tears after the mention of her mother.

"Tell me what is bothering you and we'll see if there is something we need to be concerned about. Or, maybe we can think our way through it and make it better."

Tina wiped her eyes clear. "I just want to do right by you, Velma, and Mama."

"I think I know you well enough. Are you planning on killing someone?"

Tina laughed. "No. You said you and Mama wanted us, as women, to have a chance at new opportunities."

"Yes, that's something we talked about when Velma was born and reconfirmed when you came along. I won't go into stories, but that was always our desire and our challenge. Let me tell you something I don't think you know. Something that Velma keeps quiet about. When your mother died, she was learning to be a brick mason."

"What? Really? The Guild Masters would have been furious."

"Yes, they were. Some still are. So, if there is something you think worth doing, you have to be willing to take the chance for a better opportunity. That is how your mother thought. That is how I think. And that is how you have been raised."

He picked up their bowls and poured the soup back into the pot. "Tonight looks like a good night for talking, and we'll keep the soup warm until we're done. Me, I'm happy because Lud filled in as the job foreman today, so I'm going to be working on the big house again tomorrow. You can tell me what you're so tight about."

Tina got up and went to her basket and pulled out a flyer. She unfolded it and handed it to her father.

"This group. They're having a meeting tomorrow night, and I think I want to go. They call themselves Suffragettes."

Daniel Yocom

Daniel Yocom does geeky things at night because his day job won't let him. This dates back to the 1960s through games, books, movies, and stranger things better shared in small groups. He's written hundreds of articles about these topics for his own blog, other websites, and magazines after extensive research along with short stories. His research includes attending conventions, sharing on panels and presentations, and road-tripping with his wife.

Time to Go

by Terra Luft

Content warning: abuse, violence, death

Tiny sliver at the edge
Of a covered window
Not light really
But a contrast of color
Marking the passage
Of another day
Another week
Time distilled to monotony
Broken by nightmares
She measured existence
By light that wasn't light
Slowly morphing
Blending hues
Of gray and gloom

When she wasn't alone
Her mind retreated
Focused beyond the cage
Willing herself to ignore
The throbbing in her shoulders

IF NOT NOW, *WHEN?*

From contorted bondage
Her hair matted with blood
Stiffly hanging in her eye
The roughness of fabric under her cheek
Though none covered her body
The dryness of her mouth contrasted
With the wetness oozing beneath her
From where she ached
Her lips cracked in patterns
Like the desert floor in summer

She lay broken
Exactly as he left her
Mostly dead
Like the not light
He always came
The inevitability
His fervor
His relentlessness
Hope drained
With the life
And fluid
From her body

Last spark of defiance
Awoke inside her
An ancient magic
Slowly uncurled
From deep within
Unyoked her essence
From the physical
Drew her out
Promised sunrise

Time to Go

Sunset
Where the light slivered

Go now or be lost forever
This leaving brought
A different existence
As something intangible
Soaring free
Beyond the window
Last light of the setting sun
Consumed the sky
Burnished colors in its wake
Exactly as she had conjured
The unknown beckoned
The void awaited
And welcomed her

Terra Luft

"Terra Luft is a speculative fiction author whose imagination conjures mostly dark tales, even when she tries not to. Her work explores women's themes and challenging societal norms in hopes of allowing fresh perspectives to emerge.

Terra holds a BA in Creative Writing and English from Southern New Hampshire University with a minor in Communications. She is a member of Sigma Tau Delta International English Honor Society, and The League of Utah Writers where she serves as a member of the board as a chapter president and Web Chair. She lives in the mountains of Utah with her husband and daughters."

The Wild Bunch Barber

by Bryan Young

"You a dentist?" asked the cowboy with piercing blue eyes as he took the wooden stairs up to my humble shop.

"I'm a barber," I told him. That didn't mean anything to him or his red-headed companion.

The fella with a rust-colored mustache and hair to match had his jaw swelled on one side and he held it tight as though that'd do anything for the pain. I coulda been the King of Siam for all he cared as long as I could fix his aching tooth.

"Well, surely you do some fixin' up of people now and again," the blue-eyed cowboy said, pointing to the front of my shop. "Leastways, that's what your pole says."

He was right. I had all the stripes for fixing cuts and bandaging people up, but with Doc Calloway in town, the need for me to do that sort of thing had dried up like the river. "Doc Calloway's place is just up on the hill, and I think he'd be more than happy to oblige you fellas if you went up that way. He's a mite better at that sort of thing than I am."

The blue-eyed cowboy who did the talking smiled broadly. He seemed an amiable sort. "I mean, we're short on time, and it's just a simple extraction I'd bet.

You understand, right?"

The man with the toothache moaned as they backed me farther toward the entrance of my barbershop.

"We'll make it worth your while."

While that was a nice enough gesture, I figured I'd've helped the poor fella anyway, because that's just the sort I am. Generous to a fault and kind as a kitten. I nodded my head back to the open door and sighed. "Fine. Come on in."

I turned and went in, proud of the shop I'd built. Two chairs meant I could leave a hot towel on one fella while I shaved another. A polished tin mirror ran along one wall, and the sunlight—especially in the morning like now—poured into the place like honey. The wooden floors and walls soaked it up with a gleam.

A shelf with all my instruments sat beneath the oil lamps and thin strips of horse-hide dangled from the shelf and each chair. "Why don't you have your friend take a seat just there," I said, pointing to the seat at the back.

If this fella's tooth spurted a lot of blood, that seat was closest to the water pump where the tubs were.

"Nice place you got here," the blue-eyed cowboy said, waving his hat across the shop as he regarded it.

"Many thanks, stranger. I do my best."

"It's the sort of place that makes a fella want to come and bathe."

"That's the idea."

The stricken man in the gray-blue jacket ambled toward the chair, then collapsed into it like he couldn't support his weight any longer. I hadn't dealt with a tooth that painful in a long time. Teeth were never my specialty, but I knew my way around a pair of pliers.

I left the cowboys in the front room while I went to collect my tools from the back. I put the pliers, a smattering of cotton, the ether, and a rag in the front of my apron and searched for my oldest cape. No sense in getting blood on the nicest one.

"It's fine," the talker said soft to his friend. Maybe he figured I couldn't hear. "We'll get it taken care of, lickety-split. Then we'll make the opening, no problem."

The patient groaned. Maybe there were words in there, but I couldn't make 'em out.

"No, you'll be fine. Good as new. This is gonna go easy as anything." The cowboy's voice was as smooth as my shave and well-oiled. Like he'd be able to talk anybody into anything. I figured that's why they wore irons on their hips. He'd've had to butter the sheriff up like a Christmas goose to get into town without having to surrender their pieces.

That or they were up to something nefarious.

The one in the chair said something that sounded a lot like incredulity.

"Have I ever led you wrong?"

Was that a laugh of sarcasm through the pain?

I came back into the room. My boots clicked sharp against the wood, announcing my return.

"So, it'll be a dollar and a half for the extraction," I said, spreading the cape over the ailing gentleman and the six-shooter sitting in his lap. His eyes widened a bit when he saw me eyeing it, but I didn't mention it. "Least, a dollar-fifty is what I charged when I used to do it often."

"That's a fair price," the cowboy said, clapping his hands in front of him.

I felt a "but" coming on.

And I was right.

"But," he said, "to tell the truth, he and I ain't got a penny to rub together between us at the moment."

"I see," I said, finishing up the knot in the cape at the back of the fella's neck.

"But I'll tell ya what," the cowboy said, rubbing his hands together. "We're fixin' to make some real money today and we'll make you whole. Ya just have to take my word for it."

I narrowed my eyes at the cowboy, skeptical.

He raised a hand like he was swearin' on a Bible. "On my honor. We wouldn't take a thing like this lightly. And, like I said, you'd get your due and proper. You'd just need to fix him up and let us get it first."

"You got a job in town?" I asked.

"Somethin' like that. But he can't do it with that damned toothache of his. It's just too bad." The cowboy fished a watch on a chain from his pocket, checked the time, and tsked. "And we're just running low on time is all."

I debated in my mind. I looked from the fella in the chair to the fella doin' the talking, back and forth, searchin' for an answer. The look of agony on the poor guy's face, the swell of his cheek, and the moans he issued were enough to sway my heart. If I've said it before, I'll say it again: I'm generous to a fault and kind as a kitten.

I didn't take an oath like any sort of doctor, but when a person comes to you in pain, you do your best to fix 'em up. It's just a human thing to do, right? "All right. But you'll oblige me by fillin' out an IOU, if that meets your approval."

"More than happy, more than happy. It'll only be a

formality, though, because you'll be getting your money, plus a little bonus, today."

An extra nickel on the fee would be enough to make me happy.

"If you want to get to work on him," the fella said, walking over to the counter at the front of my shop, "I'll draft up an IOU."

"There's a ledger with paper in the top drawer, a pencil, too," I told him.

He went to work on the proper paperwork while I stood over his distressed friend, readying a rag for the ether.

"No, no ether," said the talker from the other side of the room.

"What?"

"No, he, uh, he doesn't react well to it."

I couldn't even imagine the pain he'd be in if'n I yanked that son of a bitch tooth without anything to put him at ease against the pain. Just the thought of feeling the pliers on tooth enamel without the juice was enough to make me cringe.

I looked down at the patient and his wide and frightened eyes told me everything I needed to know.

If I hadn't've been able to figure it on my own, his growling, lock-jawed pleas woulda·filled me in. "Ether . . ." he said from one side of his mouth.

But the smooth-talker came over, smiling like anything, hand raised toward his friend. "Now, you know we've got to do this job, and you're not gonna be able if you're stumbling around like a jackass on ether. I need you sharp."

The man in the chair refused to make eye contact with his friend. His eyes watered just a bit as he clenched his jaw and put pressure on the offending tooth.

"He says he wants the ether," I said, going back to dousing the rag.

"No, we can't do that." He pulled his watch again, then he dangled the face in the direction of his friend. "I'm sorry, but we're outta time. If you wanna get this done beforehand, you're gonna have to do it now. No ether, nothin'."

The poor bastard shook his head.

"Listen, mister," I told his friend, "He wants the ether."

"Wantin' ain't havin', and he knows he can't."

The man in the chair closed his eyes as his friend got closer.

"Listen, you know we've got work to do. And I wouldn't ask you to do this if we didn't. But you're the one who needed this and I didn't balk. I said it would be a bad idea, and we should wait, but you said it hurt too bad. Now I told you if you wanted the ether, we could wait, but you're the one who said you couldn't. So do you want to let the man do his work and get on our way or not?"

The fella in the chair growled like a whining pup and I couldn't blame him with the way his jaw was swelled. It looked ready to pop. I hadn't even got a look at the tooth yet and I knew it was a monster.

"Efff . . ." was the noise he made.

"What was that?" his friend asked, holding his hand to his ear.

"FFuhhh . . ." he said this time.

The fella in the chair took a breath in and clenched again to speak, tears streamin' down his face. "I said . . fine . . ."

"See? Now he's talkin' sense." The cowboy looked to me with a smile. "So, you just get in there and pull that damn thing out, then we'll be on our way and you'll be a mite richer soon as can be."

I furrowed my brow. "Well, all right. If that's the way you both want it."

It didn't make too much difference to me. Sure, he'd be a bit more still on the ether, but it was more for him than anybody.

The man in the chair rolled his eyes and braced himself, gripping the arms with white knuckles like he was dangling from a roof.

"You ready, then?"

He nodded his head and kept his eyes shut.

I stuffed the bottle of ether back into my apron pocket and withdrew the pliers. They were a sturdy pair and would do the trick fast.

He didn't need to see anything and I told him so. I tried calming him as best I could, but I don't know how anyone in their right mind coulda stayed calm knowing what was about to happen.

"You need a drink?"

He nodded his head profusely, so I went to the counter and fixed him a slug of whiskey and brought it back fast. He sipped at it through his clenched teeth. Brown liquid dripped down his stubbled chin.

"Take it all in," I told him and he did. He handed the glass back and I placed it on the shelf in front of the mirror.

"I'm gonna need you to open up, now, stranger."

He parted his lips but left his jaw tightened. I knew that feeling. The one where you're puttin' pressure on the pain and the second that pressure leaves, you just feel like the pain is gonna be so bad that you're gonna float away like a dandelion and want to just jump because it hurts so damn bad. That's why he didn't want to let go of the grip he had on that tooth.

"I know it hurts, but I'm gonna need to get you to open a little wider than that. I need to see the tooth afore I can take it out."

He grumbled some as his teeth parted, but there on the bottom I could see the swell around one of the molars, half black with rot. It needed to come out something fierce and no part of it was gonna feel good. "Yeah, that one looks like it's been treatin' you like a son of a bitch for a while, hasn't it?"

He squeaked with pain, but couldn't make a more intelligible sound. He nodded his head though, which told me I had the long and the short of it.

"Now, I'm gonna put this in your mouth, I'm gonna grip it tight, and I'm gonna pull like hell. It's gonna hurt, you get me? Like, more than anything you've ever felt. You been shot?"

The fella in the chair shrugged and shook his head tightly again. He'd definitely been shot.

"It's gonna feel like that. But the difference is this gets better pretty instantly. You're gonna be sore, but not like you are now. And by tomorrow or the day after, you'll be grateful you came. Now, are you ready?"

He shook his head and closed his eyes, opening his mouth even wider.

"Good, just like that," I told him.

Turning the pliers over, I eased them into his mouth, eyeing carefully the spot I needed to clamp. I didn't want to tighten the pliers down on it until the last possible second and I wanted to give him as much warning as

I could. Even just touching the thing was going to hurt and I didn't want him squirreling beneath me. Were he to buck the wrong way, it'd cause us both a lotta hurt.

"You ready? I'm gonna do it now. You're gonna have to keep still, for both our sakes, else this is gonna hurt a lot worse. You get me?"

He closed his eyes tighter and gripped the armrests of the chair like they were the only path to holy salvation.

"Here we go, fella."

I crunched the pliers down on the tooth. Even through the handle, I felt the grit and heard the crunch against what little enamel there was left.

I counted as I slowly added pressure to my grip.

"One," I told him, the pliers tightening in my hand.

"Two," I said, squeezing harder.

The poor fella's eyes leaked through his shut lids and his fingers looked like they might break, they gripped the chair so tight.

"Three."

I wrenched the tooth out.

Blood dripped from it against the white cape.

I could never quite get used to the screams when they happened. The blood drained from his face and the poor bastard took on a cadaverous pallor like he'd lost a gallon of blood rather than just a tooth. His hands shot to his mouth and held it. But even then, the swelling was already going down in his cheek.

"See?" his buddy said. "I told you it wouldn't be so bad. You're all correct now and we'll, uh, we'll just be on our way."

I looked at the tooth, held tight in the mouth of the pliers, dripping blood. "He might need a minute."

The talkative one plucked his watch from his pocket

again and tapped on the face. "Well, a minute is something he doesn't have. Thanks again, doc."

I untied the bloody cape from his neck and uncovered him, but he made no move to stand. Not until his friend helped him to his feet and got his gun back in its holster.

"I told ya you'd get through that just fine," his friend said. "That was a helluva thing. Never seen anything like it. You took it like a champion."

The cowboy with blue eyes turned to me as his buddy shuffled to the door. "I knew you'd come through for us. Thanks for that. And I promise you'll get what's coming to you."

"You'll need this," I said, pulling the fluff of cotton from my apron.

"Oh, right," the talker said.

The poor fella turned to me and took the cotton.

"You'll want to pack it in tight and let it soak up the blood. Until it stops bleeding, anyway. Don't want to swallow too much."

He braced himself, closed his eyes, and stuffed the cotton in his bloodied mouth.

"Much obliged," he said, muffled through the anguish and the cotton.

They left as fast as they came, and I wondered what it was they were doing to earn their money. I didn't think too hard about it. I went about cleaning up the shop. I dropped the tooth in a tin and washed the pliers in one of the tubs and returned it to the shelf.

The gunshots were distant, from the other side of the main street. When the firing got closer, I went for the shotgun under the counter. I didn't know what the trouble was, but I had a guess. Being caught unawares would have been a damn foolish thing, and the last thing

I wanted to be was a damn fool.

The shooting stopped and I heard a whole pile of shouting. A horse whinnied. People were running. The sheriff barked some orders, and I gripped my shotgun even tighter.

Creeping up to the front window, I snuck a peek. Dust kicked up from the firefight and gun smoke filled the street. The scent of gunpowder hit me and I knew it had gotten too close for comfort.

That's when the back door creaked open.

"Who is that?" I shouted.

Leapin' to my feet, I hightailed it to the back just in time to see the door close again.

"Hello?"

But there was no one to be seen. I aimed the shotgun in at each tub, wondering if somebody coulda been hiding in one of them, but both were empty.

"Anybody?"

Somebody had to have opened the door.

And that's when I noticed it, sitting in front of the back door.

A big rock holdin' down some paper.

It looked like a page from my ledger.

Walking over, I kicked the rock over with my boot. The IOU.

And beneath it, two crisp ten-dollar bills.

I turned the IOU over to find a note written on the back. "Couldn't have done it without ya. —Butch"

"Well, I'll be a damned fool."

Bryan Young

Bryan Young works across many different media. His work as a writer and producer has been called "filmmaking gold" by The New York Times. He's also published comic books with Slave Labor Graphics and Image Comics. He's been a regular contributor for the Huffington Post, StarWars.com, Star Wars Insider magazine, SYFY, /Film, and was the founder and editor in chief of the geek news and review site Big Shiny Robot! He co-authored Robotech: The Macross Saga RPG in 2019 and in 2020 he wrote a novel in the BattleTech Universe called Honor's Gauntlet. He teaches writing at conferences across the country and at the University of Utah. He teaches courses for Writer's Digest University as well. He's also active with the League of Utah Writers as president of the Salt City Genre Writers and President-Elect of the League itself. Follow him on Twitter @swankmotron.

About the Monkeys

by Johnny Worthen

This year, 2021, sees the sixth year of the infamous Infinite Monkeys Chapter of the League of Utah Writers. Its full name is, "LUW Genre Writers - Infinite Monkeys." We call ourselves "The Monkeys" for short. (Hey hey.) The Monkeys were the first official niche chapter in the League's history, specifically designed for speculative fiction as opposed to literary, it actually embraced writing in any genre, which is, really, anything.

It was a groundbreaking chapter in the League's history for its specialty and its kinship. Assembled February 3, 2016, it was overtly formed to create a safe space where writers could join in community and fellowship, practice their art, help each other, and NOT take themselves too seriously. Thus the name.

The name Infinite Monkeys refers to the famous Infinite Monkey Theorem—the idea that given enough time, a bunch of monkeys at typewriters will eventually write Hamlet. There was much debate as to the name originally—thus the super long one above—but enough of us, having suffered the slings and arrows of outrageous fortune, personal and professional, understood the need for a place of non-judgment and compromise, a place of friends, a place of mutual respect and, dare I say, love. The name is intentionally whimsical and silly, a reminder of our playful and friendly roots. It's hard to be too uptight when you liken yourself to a bonobo at a keyboard. The image makes me smile every time. We should all take it easy. If not now, when?

The Monkeys stated mission is to support our membership and help those with the goal of publication to achieve that. We create a space for writers of all levels to share knowledge and insight, new words and ideas, successes and failures. Meeting twice monthly, we offer classes and critique, write-ins, inspiration of all kinds, publication opportunities, writing retreats, fellowship, fun. Cookies sometimes. Bananas of course.

To learn more about the Infinite Monkeys, visit:
https://luwgenremonkeys.wordpress.com

Or on Facebook:
https://www.facebook.com/groups/LUWInfiniteMonkeys

Thanks for reading,

Johnny Worthen,
Vice President, Infinite Monkeys

About the League of Utah Writers

by John M. Olsen

As President of the League of Utah Writers, I love it when chapters put together projects like this anthology. Chapters within the League do amazing work in educating and encouraging their members as they provide opportunities to be published. You, as a reader, get to reap the benefits of their work. At least three chapters have published collections of stories or poetry just this year in addition to League-wide publications. Not only do the authors involved get experience with writing and being published, but there is also editing, layout, cover design, marketing, and the whole pipeline of publishing all the way from the first idea to having a book in their hands and the hands of their readers.

Every bit of that pathway is useful for authors who want to improve their craft, and that's what the League is about: helping writers get better at what they do, and helping them find success.

The League has been around since 1935 when Olive Woolley Burt became its first president. Ever since, the League has been dedicated to helping its members and the local writing community through networking, critiques, classes, and conferences. We recently renamed our writing awards as The Olive Woolley Burt Awards to honor Ms. Burt's contributions, both as our first president and as a prolific author who took on a range of subjects that shed light on causes and people who could benefit from her work.

Despite the wonderful opportunity to be published in this collection alongside my friends, I would say the greatest thing the League—and the Infinite Monkeys chapter—have done for me personally is to drag me kicking and screaming out of my shell. I've learned to network and make contacts with writers, editors, agents, and publishers. I've become an editor as well as an author. When you multiply that effect by hundreds of members, you begin to see the power of working together toward common goals.

There's a concept known as "zero-sum game" where there is a fixed-size pie that everyone fights over. Writing isn't like that. The success of one author does not reduce the success of another. This is what brings success to organizations like the League of Utah Writers and to chapters like the Infinite Monkeys, who put this volume together. That success passes through to our members and the community at large. If we write well enough, market it right, and get books into the hands of new readers, the market grows.

But readers are more than a market to be sold to. Each of those readers is a person—just like you, dear reader—who is entertained or influenced somehow by what we write. The world is a different place because of what we do and because of our influence on you. We may provide a bit of levity, give you a chill up the spine, or share a moment of escape from the challenges of the real world, and you are partners with us in experiencing and sharing emotions.

About the League of Utah Writers

Are you a writer? Join us! Define the success you're after and see what we can do to help you on your journey.

Are you a reader? We owe what we are to you. I hope you find a new favorite author or have found something new written by someone you already follow. That's one of the benefits of anthologies like this one: you have a sampling from several authors you don't know but might become a fan of.

Do you know a non-reader? I hope you help them find a story to fall in love with so we can make the pie bigger.

I saw a comic a few weeks back where an author and a fan met face to face for the first time. The fan was excited to meet the author who wrote the story they loved. The author was excited to meet someone who loved their work. Both were oblivious to the excited fan factor the other experienced. It really can feel like that.

We're all in this together, so let's have fun and make the most of it. Share what you love with others. We can each make a difference as we follow the theme for this collection and its call to action: If not now, when?

Few things will touch the heart of an author faster than hearing someone say, "I loved your story." This sort of success between writers and readers is what this book and the League of Utah Writers are all about.

John M. Olsen,
President, League of Utah Writers